TRINITY & ITS TWIN

POETRY BY HARAMBEE GREY-SUN

Spring's Fall (Autumn Numbers * Book I)
Wine Songs, Vinegar Verses
Trinity & Its Twin

FICTION BY HARAMBEE K. GREY-SUN

Standalone Stories
Beholder
Love Among the Ultramoderns
Unfair Play
Last Contact
The Lure
Colder Than Ice

The *EVE OF LIGHT* Series

<u>The Novels</u>
BloodLight: The Apocalypse of Robert Goldner (*Prequel*)
Broken Angels (*Book I*)
Divinities, Entangled (*Book II*)

<u>The Short Stories</u>
Hell's Brood (*A Collection*)

TRINITY & ITS TWIN

A Subversive Narrative

Harambee Grey-Sun

HyperVerse Books, LLC

ACKNOLWEDGMENTS
Grateful acknowledgement is made to the editors and publishers of *RiverSedge*, where "The Last Breakfast" first appeared.

Cover design by Kelvin Reese

Cover art copyright © knssr/stock.adobe.com

Print ISBN-13: 978-1-64044-017-3

Ebook ISBN-13: 978-1-64044-018-0

Published by HyperVerse Books, LLC
P.O. Box 23642
Alexandria, VA 22304
www.hyperversebooks.com

Crossing genres without apologies.

CONTENTS

Introductory Note / 1

The Characters / 3

PROLOGUE

Amusing Disgrace / 7

PART I: THE ASCENT AND FALL

Mission Statement / 11

Small World / 12

Scraps / 14

Legacy / 15

The Other Bench / 16

Angel Ashes / 17

Extract from a City Newsmagazine Editorial / 19

Extract from a Suburban Newspaper Editorial / 20

The Last Breakfast / 22

Beggars' Request / 24

Fragments of Pragmatism / 25

Granted / 27

David's Star / 28

PART II: THE SUMMIT AND PIT

Waycross, Texas / 31

Mound Xyn / 33

The First Feast / 35

Match / 38

Extract from a Community Newspaper Editorial / 51

Jihad and Rumors of Peace / 52

Call to Arms / 54

Twister (Hanid's Lesson) / 56

The New Age of Reason (Shariah's Lesson) / 58

The Rules of Engagement / 59

Trinity Polygamy / 61

Extract from a Religious Organization's Newsletter / 63

Solomon's Seal / 65

For the Crescent to Cross the Star / 69

PART III: THE DESCENT AND SCALE

The Anthill / 73

Beside Bedside Manners / 75

Shekinah / 77

Spy to Thief / 79

Hex / 81

Salam / 86

Rehearsal (Hanid's Secret Teaching) / 88

The Scramble / 90

Age, Vent; Advantage / 92

Burning the Oil / 93

Extract from the Nation's Capital's Newspaper / 95

Cradlesong (Shariah's Private Prayer) / 97

Holocaust / 99

EPILOGUE

Extract from an Anti-Establishment Newsletter / 127

About the Author / 129

INTRODUCTORY NOTE

Begun in 1999 and finished in 2000, *Trinity & Its Twin* is, on cursory examination, a collection of dense poetry. Just under its seemingly inscrutable skin, it is a verse novel about a homeless refugee and a runaway teenager who join a religious sect, fall in love, and then seemingly lose everything. At its deepest level, it is an allusive meditation, an allegory about the synthesis of loves false and true.

An intricate work that some will find confounding and others may find rewarding, *Trinity & Its Twin*, after twenty years, may now find its audience.

THE CHARACTERS

Hanid, a refugee from a war-torn land, is a homeless antiwar activist. He worked construction in his native land and now considers himself, at his core, a poet, one who constructs new realities with words. Eventually, he is inspired to make his way to Texas where he takes refuge with a religious sect. Here, he meets Shariah, whom he considers his muse materialized.

Shariah, born to a teenage mother who left her in a refuse bin, spends years in an orphanage run by corrupt opportunists before being adopted by a seemingly loving couple. Realizing her adopted parents' interest in her have little to do with love, she runs away, guided by the voices of chanting and singing children whom only she can hear. She winds up in Texas, where she meets Hanid and David.

David, a failed musician who withdrew into himself so deeply and completely that he believed he formed a union with God, resides at the Mound Xyn Center in Texas. Here, he labors to compose his greatest piece: Armageddon. In his mind, and in the minds of his followers, he is the One, manifested in the flesh. Any who wish to be truly saved must make the pilgrimage to Xyn and submit to his will.

PROLOGUE

AMUSING DISGRACE

Surrender to this Grade.

In the name of self-Love
(the kind kid-forbidden,
but for a lonely wife, forgiven),
I bear witness that there is not a Satan of hate,
no damning demons, but only Adam—men
and women abusing excusing accusations, mating
sensations, pretending to conceive bliss, intending
morning-after sickness.

Come to me: distant nozzle-kiss,
reincarnated as a mist-embrace;
replace these dull older sin cells, pushed outward;
reveal the younger layer of sky; the night,
washed.

I bear morning witness no serpent has hissed
his way through the garden's bush.
For this mourning, the sly guard pried open
her own gates, baiting the Master (self-created)
of her twisted fate. Lonely vigil, waxing
without candles for a clean, healthy, shiny
atonement.

Come from me: the ignorance
of insolent innocence. The autoerotic
genesis of hypnotic genius: There is no
rational reason behind this creation:
Black-hole expulsions; pulsating
messages, massaging; speaking spitless,
wording witless; spatter, sputter in unintelligible
tongues—eligible for an entrance into holy hell.

In the Names (sixty-three sexed
dirty with thirty-six) of the Truth refined,
in infinite glories, stories to be sung
in unity, hymned with praise, ominous

promises of no impunity for the usual world
of anti-sensualists (I'm obliged
by my obloquies), I bear witness there is no Truth
but that in which I trust.
This is better than the omens
seen after bedside amens.

Surrender to this Grace.

PART I:
THE ASCENT
AND FALL

MISSION STATEMENT

Mission of mayhem—may they repair
    such a frail frame,
    a cripple on one crutch
    supporting a lucrative venture?

Sinister Mercy—who will rescue the fish drowning
    under leaky roofs? Pails overflowing; suddenly,
    I long for my gutters—alternative habitat
    for the indignant.   Whom did I emulate
    to deserve this immolation?

But, my snide remarks bite past the bark
of this tree of life. Repugnant and untidy
surroundings can do without my rowdy impugning.

Medicine mission—minimum portions of onion stew
    dished out by minions
    in return for tasks, menial,
    overdue.

Some unscrew the flasks, but windows go unsealed;
    curtains, unmended; furniture spurned by hammer and nail.
    The furnace (my assignment) keeps the warmth.
    That's an earned check for work ethic;
    but, the lover of Phosphor hides the light
    that might
    make us all prosper.

Thunder's blunder—the rain rushed in
    with an officers' parade,
    pale blues on a crack raid.
    Is this how my prayers are paid?

Rescued by the Law which saw Mercy's ministers as thugs
smuggling drugs, using us homeless as a clueless front.
Only too proud to testify, act as a witness, against dealers
(blind killers) by my home
on the corner.

SMALL WORLD

Remembering foregone presentations:
forlorn, back to this cracked sidewalk, alone.
Recognition made under sensations,
tingly, skin crawling. Unplugged telephone.

Who had I to call at that stagnant age?
No matter. No service; overdue rent.
Fellow quartered boarders could spare no cent.
Age pared of consent, how would we share change?

Back in those times when the skies spat acid
and the faucets cried rancid solutions,
some prayed that our small world would turn placid—
placebo pills drunk with destitution.

Our overseers insisted on this:
"The bums of the earth are, in truth, God's chums.
The status of a child is a plus. Slums
will be scoured at Judgment: Fields of bliss."

Six years, ferment, in the splits of pavement,
green-weed revolution struggles fiercely
to gain on God's war against enslavement.
"Wars are fought to switch tyrants"—sticks pierce me.

Dignity stripped, physically and in mind.
Obtuse abuse. Who knew violets red-bleed?
Could tell nonfiction before I could read;
"molest" ushered a dictionary-find.

Who cared for the orphans locked in a war
raging in a shelter funded by aid,
coins funneled from well-wishers through State doors
who blocked our sun, locked our growth, got gold-paid?

Inside camp: black and grey televisions
with less than five channels; patches on eyes;

one fan; rusty toys. Rustic enterprise—
thatched roofs; stitched walls; hitched bulls tell derisions.

Only occupations changed our stations.
Left the tent once a week to meet the streets.
Yield signs read child labor violations—
but our masters knew chore detours, discreet.

Two meals a day came our way dependent
upon our talent to perform, warming
the souls of the cold commuters swarming,
noses up—the scents of the indignant.

Some played flutes, triangles, or bucket drums;
others whistled, snapped fingers, tapped a shoe.
What drew claps, clangs of change, from rubes rubbed dumb
were the vocals I belted out in blue.

Sincere, true, as we were always hungry.
To eat, we each had to "buy" our own seat.
Sharing, children ate the socialist meat:
"Yearn, move—you'll quit your status as 'young, free.'"

Providence came—guises: goose and gander,
two Born-Agains seeking restitution
for overpaid sin fees. Seers squander.
"Buy for kids? Not in the constitution."

Adopted at six: excused from the trench.
Pass to present: upon the cracked cement
stage where we harangued for our government,
diverting money from men on the bench.

SCRAPS

Sheets of paper—
old news to me.
Bedded down on a cardboard carpet
in a storm, but plenty warm; arms wrapped in rags.
Nappy hair—pillow for naps here or there.
Stomach settled with brunch scrounged:
a fat rat's garbage, a mendicant's nourishment.
Objects digesting objects rejected . . .
but (if they pay attention at all) we're sold as menaces, worthless?

I rest contented. Rather than scraps
between two, three, or more, I prefer that which feeds
a living scrapbook, helping others remember the horrors of terrors.
Cozy in my nook, developing graphs, seeking wisdom, still,
to understand why national objectives are so rarely objective
and primarily promote national suicide.

Once developed homes in another land,
one engulfed in a civil dispute over boundaries, languages, flag colors.
Although neutral, grey, we were pictured as residing, hiding
on the black side of the fray by Allies, alien interventionists.
Meddlers for peace, publishing tarnishings,
launching daily and weekly bombings—how to prevent
the Force for Justice's accident?

The Blood of Abraham in one body, on one course, spilt; split.
Alive: One survivor of five, left to stumble over the mystic
mish-mashed mouthed word jumble: dismembering bodies of families
for national unity is a part in promoting international civil stability.
I remember nothing but being dispossessed of homestead memories.
Headed from a shack, reduced to matchsticks, burning rubble,
I crossed the ocean, kissed the shore as an immigrant,
expected to be welcomed with arms bearing materials to help me
rebuild my splintered dreams. My cheers were allayed when I came
to know the scraps of my Allies' liberating land:
   "Pull away from the domestics

        so, elsewhere, we may give a hand."

LEGACY

Moms and dads: proms for pre-grads
are polluted with such
dreamers amongst streamers
sprinkling angels' dust—
peppering premonitions of promotions.

Sneeze; sweep to the sides,
dancing in negligees,
tornados, negligent
concerning the skin they brush away,
rubbing shoulders in careless orgies.

Rubbish: gratuitous congratulations
for aspirations yet to be achieved.
Exaggerations, fueled by excessive libations,
instill illusions of physical prowess
in the other sex.
Lost in extravagance,
bellies and chests rub, producing more dust.

Litter born. Cats who seek to be fat
have no time for a child's play. Thrown away:
Chaste babe dumped in a basket for waste,
rescued by the State
and placed with a lawful family;
recycled ash-can foundling.

At this crux of fifteen—
birthday suite cakes—it's crucial I break the hypocrisy
legacy of present and future authorities.
This year, won't even bother with candles.

Light the leaves.
Leaving light.

THE OTHER BENCH

Can't figure out who clutches their purses tighter
to their sides, the duller or the brighter?
Skin color's no determinant for this thought:
". . . bench bugs will spend it on liquor or drugs."

Not so discriminating when supporting foreign excursions,
wasting lives, resources, in civil feuds; diversions
from homegrown challenges. Patriots over sugar hills.
Warmongers singing no longer for life, liberty, but pursuits . . .

Silent vagabond, I neither beg nor ask;
I'm a victim of my and others' free will,
choice of voice, reacting actions.
Low tolerance for self-pity's stench
wafted after the garbage is washed ashore,
drafted, drifting on waves; grafting the daft,
appealing to loyalty.
Self-serving tokens; self-loving sluts, but hypocritical slots;
such inhuman machines. Phosphor's smokescreens.

Engage to assuage the guilt of a riddled conscience,
to cure another nation's diseases. Here, avoidance
to maintain that sanguine mind-state while contributing
to uprooting a faraway land-state through means sanguinary.

"Ma'am, I detect you detest your own moroseness, as you're
an unbled, but an undoubtedly remorseful, casualty of these wars.
I insist you take these roses, free of charge"—spurred by nervousness,
they barge right by me as I, in my sandals, persist in my protest
against taxing scandals over patches of land, meaningless green, and
the same change that comes with it. Viewed as refuse, I refuse food,
money, and pity. I'm here as a dissident,
       but what of the veterans on the other bench?

ANGEL ASHES

School library at noon—
skipping out on lunchroom camaraderie,
rather spend this time flipping through anthologies
of poetry that sticks to my bones and
stones my heart. The analogy
would be: a cemetery roamed by a lone zombie
passed over by Izrail. Well, this library
has more than a few zombies who wear their habits
shyly, outcast by soft-spoken personalities.

My friend, seeking my apology for an earlier argument,
is the exception.

New scenario:
Kicking through the doors: Two unlearned classical liberals
who also oppose the mandatory lunch program,
equating public schools with bullying pogroms.

One, with a shotgun, aims it dead,
blasts through the librarian's head.
His companion enters the labyrinth of shelves,
chasing the undead who want to preserve their selves.
Me, I hide under my table
                        as if this is a tornado drill.
Glass shatters, blood spatters;
          hollers, screams, and laughs might make a blind one
mistake this as hilarious.

Apparently it is to the two delirious
          students in trench coats ignoring none.
My time has come to run—
          looking for a path clear.
My best friend, dear, shot by the spineless,
          aiming for her vertebrae.
The bangs still reverberate in my ears as I take off
for the direction most silent:
A back corner, sunlit.

Something clicks—
                    I drop to my knees.

"Turn around slowly."

Each eye staring down a barrel.

"Give the right answer, we'll end this quarrel:
            You believe in God?"

Shaking uncontrollably, can't nod.
                            The gun is fired
from a lawful sharpshooter outside the window.

Twenty-four kids killed. Only one left undead.
The police wrap me in blankets, asking me . . . . . I can't hear
beyond uncounted shots ringing, one inquiry still stinging.
Asked by Adam, I give the answer to bless.
One word: "Yes."

Don't tell,
passing from this day, I only roam alone
till I kiss Uriel.

EXTRACT FROM A CITY NEWSMAGAZINE EDITORIAL

". . . four foreign terrorists bombed the welfare building.
Some claim the crime wave has risen proportionately
to the immigrants arriving here as refugees.
Following, as in the sea,

"rioters ran rampant, setting blazes with rage,
razing stores. An inconvenience: to sack, to loot
the structures that employed them by day.
More than fired, their entire lives are soot.

"Light the blame under the Law,
the paralyzing policies of departments,
manic, allowing maniacs to run child-wild.

"Muggings are suffocating folks on the streets.
The subways feature stabbings, disturbed freak shows, no pity.
Tourists are shutting their eyes, opening
their wallets in other cities.

"My merry holiday is but paces away,
but impending violence may push me from my birthplace.
The choice: Celebrating an anniversary of celibacy
with death, or leaving the Enemy's new base.

"The city's smart citizens are
looking up to the outskirts, arming
themselves, climbing to the suburbs to protect their assets,

"whether skinny or chinny; it's not all about wealth.
But health is a factor. It's preservation.
Good schools, strong families, caring neighborhoods—
now we natives seek reservations
in our own land . . . granted, we've stolen; but, hey,
history must end some day!"

EXTRACT FROM A SUBURBAN NEWSPAPER EDITORIAL

". . . smog blocking more rays, darkness increasing daily.
Is it a heavenly portent or reminder
of last week's school scandal and accompanying melee?
Or is God, like us, wishing He were blinder?

"Pillows of pollution, we recline on, doze off.
Godless bohemians, relocating, bring their habits.
More spouses turn to neighboring idols, taking clothes off,
while, unsupervised, their kids are impressing rabbits.

"I ask again, fellow men, what whore's war did we lose
to fall into the twin sins of child neglect, spousal abuse?
No, there's no liberty
       granted by me
for women who cheat,
       urchins sassing in the streets.
But, if we're splitting hairs,
       divvying up cares,
           finding perfect faults,

"let's start with the mayor and his cronies' apathy
at blocking the path of other cities' fugitives.
How are we to live in an overcrowding, ever-loudening
town going down the Lordless lane of brimstone?
The impolite urbanites have aroused one passion within them:
To pass a new curfew law forbidding walks at night.
Martial law marching to outlaw our favorite marital pastime.

"Dim disposition?
       In an old-fashioned mold?
Say I'm too angry?
       That was my church burning,
bombed days before the school shooting.
       Rooted, we grew in peace.
          The tide's turning . . .

"What can you do, families, but your own duty,
God-given? Reclaim your kin: spouses, parents, children.

Disobey any who order you to sacrifice, to benefit the many,
pennies or good sense, blood relations or grass within your fence,
your private property—resist improper decrees.

"Back to the scorched fields to rebuild the churches,
declaring them strongholds against the tyranny of apathy!"

THE LAST BREAKFAST

Turning over
a cracked egg, sunny side down;
nothing easy going over on this Sunday,
mourning the starvation, deprivation of sleep.
They shake me from my nighttime nirvana
to consume their artificial manna.

This is the farcical, official family-fattening time
before I'm coerced off to church for an execution
of my joyless duties to the ployful community.

Pass the fried ham, bologna;
roll the jellies over here. They start the morn
with sinfully sweet cheer
to make up for their queries, pelting me
for breaking last night's curfew, making a break
from their routine Saturday night quarrels
about whose duty it is to get a better job
in order to stuff the extra mouth. A silent body
is one well-fed,
or dead.

Force-feeding with pitchforks: "This dish of food
is for your own good."
The minister communicated as much
with altared words before cutting the cord, drying off
the newborns, newly wed to the fundamentals
in their heads. Common law—To get into heaven,
there's a grocery list of what to buy, what to offer,
what to bleed, what to feed
to a manic-depressive Spirit.

For mother's nighttime sins of omission, she drinks
the morning gin of commission, syrupy (sugar water,
thicker than blood), usurping power
with frantic rantings;
disrobed, slippers flipped off, her rise
is stifled by a cough

brought on when father attempts to forcibly sedate her
with pitted dates.
> *Pitiless. She spits the flesh out, continues on.*

Runny arguments—seasoning with salt, garlic, pepper,
powdered sugar makes these meals inedible. Delicious
superstitions, like rich, decadent chocolate gravy
escorting butterscotch biscuits with peanut butter and rum
pancakes (flipped, flapjacks) past my lips . . . indulgence.
The nectar of reason washed down the spread . . . incredible.

But while sinking in violence,
I'm thinking in silence:
> *The system can be cleaned out,*
> *but my memory's records are indelible.*

BEGGARS' REQUEST

On the worst of bad days—a Friday—
the poor forcemen of the preposterous
accost me, with curiosity for my history,
the unseen payers of my fees for my vocal job
of distracting sympathy from their silent pleas.

A traitor, infiltrator, collaborator, or spy:
Lies of allies . . . or, better, associates
who hate me in earnest.

A beggar's arrest
involves no reading of rights, only a choice.
Accusing, they try to shuttle me to and from wings,
left and right. I'm no cock, but I fear I might have to fight.

What true vagrant would engage in such flagrant ploys,
making patrons annoyed, distrustful, suspicious of the rest?
A rat to detest for his art of protest.

Those who refuse dollars, instead choosing change, reform,
handing out literary leaflets to inform, bruise those on the asphalt
whose lives are ignored. For their dehydration,
is this Pacifist truly at fault?

Gaggle of ten and three bruise, beat . . . their unearthly methods
unearth nothing, so they choose to bury me near the sea
(where they won't have to hear or see me).

Left bleeding on the shore, the shelter of the seashells
provides little comfort. In them, I hear the roar
of the true poor accompanying fictions of crucifixions.

Unsung, among crumpled trash, broken glass,
loitering. To recycle or to bury?
A thinning "Y" of a question;
either, in the end, will fulfill
the beggars' request.

FRAGMENTS OF PRAGMATISM

Thicket beyond. Roads branching off three ways.
Three results—All to end in unity, one, or
each one to end in infinity?

Proportionate to no light: fear.
Sightless, I hear . . .
March on to the hums.

Searching for the empirical Empire of Ideas, where ideal sensations
have reign over the body of spirited children of the light, corporealized.
A feeling Spirit; one to touch, hear and respond
to grievances, giving security, solace, laces
that hitch. Hiking on.

The defaced traces of solicitors.
Mindful of encouragement. Keep an eye out.
Instrumentally, accompany me.

Requiring the acquirement of land, promised by these
disembodied voices, a children's choir of
twenty-four. Practical acts for facts—
reaction to invincible invisibilities,
slavers of salvation, lies to keep
the kids, the servants in line.
Voices of Treason, for propaganda purposes only.
Trust; a safe higher learning experience.
Learn; obey civil disobedience.

Ensemble; sounds, multiplying. Prolific thoughts.
Valueless, less an outcome. Tangible angels.
Sympathy taken upon a thumb.

This religious vehicle, van parked on a little lot,
gassing to pass through several states.
Runaway, riding for a ways, a way to effect
the moment into a movement.
Fated to be free; moccasins on my feet.
Distracted by abstract structures made perfect

by incomplete but practical
speculations about possible feats
when God's Truths and Nature's Theory meet.

Further on . . .
Hums to drums, snapping thumbs,
generous notes off unseen generative tongues:
"Bring gifts; talents—proof of existence."

Nondescriptive adjectives of plural
nouns announced spontaneously,
exploded, crumbled, jumbled into a sum,
one mass resembling a parti-colored sun.
My cosmic guide. My transport to a higher life.

The Creative Spirit, to be fleshed (to keep an eye on),
to be flushed out from hiding by pithy sayings to forget never.
Hear suggestions, two of ten:
"Adhere to useless values, never again."
"Perfection, achieved with the right balance of sins."
Audible clarity, won;
now, visually, on to the One of ubiquity . . .

GRANTED

Granted
and put to misuse:
land for researchers to study myth's brain food.

Granted
wishes of free green,
fish for nourishment. Forget the experiment—erosion.

One-liter bottles littering the beach,
discarded by wish-spent men dispirited
by their jinn, taken for granted.
Parting waves; moving to avoid closer shaves.

Granted,
art's unwanted here.
Hearts burn on the spicy recipes for peace.

Granted:
damp, it looked like mine—
pamphlet of poetry I handed out to passersby.

I'll be no party to the perverse brats spitting down
on their Mother. Free-verse and cigarette butts stuffed
in some of these bottles, but . . . reverse . . .
Whose white lines are these?

"Wayward soul," it reads, "the God of Peace you search for
requests your presence in the West . . ." Granted.
It's the right light-saving time to make a curious pilgrimage
beyond the sand and the seas.

DAVID'S STAR

A fallen soul's wish at God's candle, snuffed out
by a silent wind helping the child of arisen Children
about her way.
Tried to train my voice with the aid of the chorus,
but attempted magic incantations have just left me hoarse.

What to say when I arrive at my destination,
weary with anticipation,
to meet the Word who has taken flesh?

The silent wind helps along the way
on the line of black stars, in the sea;
one seems golden, illuminating
the path to life and reconstruction.
What wisdom, instruction, would the dim stars give
if I had the time-space to listen?

*

It's been written: "God sighed; breath manifested
as frost, condensed down into the dust, mixed,
with a flash, became flesh."
This, I must witness.

Could it be even more glorious than that star, flaring,
surnamed "Freedom" following "Peace"?
Some place themselves in, travel by constellations;
right now, I've more faith in these rickety boxcars.

Heavens expanding, earth shrinking away;
eventually there'll be a watery reunion,
ending Creation's trial separation.
Until then, how am I to deal with the dual forces
tugging at reality—The Truth of the matter
and a spiritual: "Let It Be"?

PART II:
THE SUMMIT
AND PIT

WAYCROSS, TEXAS

Crossing the bridge over gorgeous waters
waving me into the arms of a small halcyon town,
I'm stirred to recall a city, long lost . . .

Hopping off the cattle car, my sandals kiss
the end-travel gravel as my eyes spy the sign, confirming:

"Welcome to Waycross,
the geographical heart of the Lone Star State."
A modest enter sign for a place of such entrancing design.

To my right, down the curving avenue of the river,
the vista reveals no less than a fertile crescent,
teeming with verdant life, exorbitant.

Hobbling along the riverwalk, eye-shopping with the currency
of the mind, I attempt to patronize every stop in the gallery,
on each side and underfoot. But what are they selling?
It seems they're taking in: On one side, a rich bank;
on the other, currents of silver; and underneath me,
pebbles finer than most gemstones.

Starving, perhaps I should be foraging for food
among the foliage, on the waters, or in the underbrush.
Fauna I've yet to see, hear or even sense,
save for the plethora of squirrels and waterfowls;
but I've no heart to eat them.

As my guides, wherever they dart or glide, my gape follows
and, behold, there's something new, hitherto unnoticed.
The tour fee is for me to let everything be.

Up onto the bank (once under water), into the luxuriant
floral variety, a mallard waddles. Without hesitation, I go behind
this creature who's laid down, taken sympathy upon a dullard—me.

On hands and knees, groveling to bypass short, thick trees,
I come into a primeval place: a park uninhabited by hoboes

or dregs and their habituations.

Immobile at first, until, to my left, I spot a trash can.
Wondering what use wildlife has for a garbage bin,
I limp over and take a gander in.

When scratches mismatch itches, there's a feeling
opposite to the one I experience now as I retrieve
from the barrel a flyer with directions
to a community with free meals and lodging.

I exhibit the paradoxed box of calm enthusiasm
of a heartlander expatriate who, searching for
a shorter route to Aesthesia's spices, has turned the curve
and seen possibilities firm in the green vista.

MOUND XYN

The Children chanted, chided, riding me
outside the "ex," marking the spot of discontents,
unfulfilled in their selfish quests;
a settlement of some who've come
to gain mastery of the shared mystery:

Centered on the sprawling earth, upon a mound, the lost
but undaunted Children found a sanitary, sanctified compound.
Home on a ranch, on the fringe of a branch, a Family
of friends sits on acres (seventy and seven) consecrated "Xyn"—
commune of elitist separatists who feel, see God's presence
here in Real and labor to translate him to the dry and icy world.

"Xynism," the Children inform, "is distinctionism."
Here's an enclave for like minds that feel all but are still alone;
small society choosing the power of piety,
disavowing self-pity, seeking intimacy with an Entity.

In reconnaissance, scanning the scene, I count the population, free,
noticing that there are three diverse thirds: men, women, and minors,
ranging. A mixed multitude of Asians, Caucasians, Latinos, and Africans,
diasporaed—all, except the patriots of myopia, are welcome.
Red, white, and black single star atop the pole, unmapped, flapping,
waving in all wayward winds from the reaches of continents.

Never before seen that starred flag,
straining now to see the stripes;
still, in some dim recognition,
I feel exuberance, numbing pain.

Woozy from the elation . . . concentration straying, splaying abroad across
the globe, garnishing cruel meals of gruel, mush for shrunken stomachs.
Inspired by Some or One to clothe the globe's juvenilely naïve,
knaves and slaves in robes of mutual self-awareness.

I pray aloud in lyrics or verses, dousing sinful, cynical curses, thankful
to know God has lost none, save those who choose to lose themselves.

The voice of choice, I've ceded control over my larynx to the Children who've brought me to Xyn to labor for a global-powerful Peace.

THE FIRST FEAST

Pay a prayer to the One who spread that beautiful array
before me, bountifully blessed that the Lord (beneficent, merciful
and meticulous) never passes a mess
without attempting to clean.

Mistaken as a panderer who'd meandered too far
from town; crippled sot carried by the river's ripples
in search of a day's nourishment.

As they sat me at the table's head for a communal meal
and passed the appetizer (unleavened bread), my eyes prowled
(as my stomach growled) for the scheme, the scam,
the sham,
what they were trying to hide.

If anything, it was poached fowl my eyes found, focused
on the main course: roast duck with dressing, feathers plucked;
flanked with fruits plucked from a generous
hidden tree.

Picked not too distant from the fruits' source, the flowers
made for exotic banquet bouquets, no less colorful than the folks
at my trestle table; a multinational Family, clearly anti-nuclear,
told by their appearance, their words,
the way they courteously responded
to each.

Gracious, shocked beyond eloquence,
I could only smile, nod, and wince
(as another hunger pang was dismissed).

After a dessert of a flaky-crust apple pie, my identity was studied
and clarified by only one, the deity of this community: David.

Taking the podium near the altar to preach a speech, doling out the duties
for the week, he paused after this ritual introduction and introduced me
as the messenger for whom they were previously instructed to pray.

David delivered, altering this homeless activist
into the Purifier and Replenisher upon whom
the Apocalypse
will hinge.

Grateful for the appointment,
but should even a god put such stock
in one unanointed?

The hall was lit only by seven menorahs with red, black, and white
candles making for an ambience romantic and, at the same time,
phantasmagoric. When David finished dishing out
the spiritually enhancing chores, divvied among the laborers
adult and adolescent, he descended from his lectern and approached me
in confidence, assuring that he knew me through sentience.

My moral assignment, the one for which he had summoned me
from afar, supersedes the ordinary drudgery of servile chores:
I'm to pioneer a program of purity to prepare the Family members' bodies
for spiritual maturity. Despite his hospitality to all, David said, some inhale
treachery, trying, in their impatience, to cheat their way into the empyrean
by treating themselves to drugs.

My role will be to supervise detoxification: caffeine, tobacco, cocaine
. . . the wide range.

". . . turn those with deserting spirits
into fertile pasturelands."

Finally, I divined David's design:
Prepare the Family for the Great Purification
that shall soon occur during The Beginning
. . . the approaching Beginning. Part of the preparation
had been exampled by the dietary laws observed
at this First Fruits Feast.

In my place, face spaced with peace of thought,
I joined the group in the last line.

As no drinks had been permitted with the meal,
we sealed the evening by dipping our cups

into great bowls
of grape punch.

MATCH

So you are?

As you are: Seeking to be surprised wise.
Sister . . . ?

Shariah. Peaking; too old for peeking.
I guess I've been sent to you for remodeling, counselor;
reform, minister . . . ?
I'm sorry, I guess I forgot . . .

Sharif, Brother Hanid.

Right. The master minister.

Your "Brother," Sister.

David said you might mold me, embolden.

If you can suffer my words for a few moments.
I can't give the whole shape. We must stop equal ways,
carrying our cares,
sharing sweet and sour grapes.

Sharing a whine? Confessional, out loud, eye-prying prayers?

Yes. Without inhibition or prohibition: tangling, strangling vines.
Splurging before purging.
Everyone must be drug- and alcohol-free before being born
into the Family.
Open yourself. I'll begin with it, protruding truth,
intending to spill my sins.

(The pure prurient has spit quite a bit already.
A wispy frame on a dirty, unsteady foundation, exfoliating white specks
and black checks as he sways where and there; the scraggly beard
on the cheeks and chin of this poseur can't hide his expression,
one of appearing constantly constipated.)

I came to Xyn—not naïve, hoping to believe—but on griefs
and relieving beliefs already living within. From the Middle East
to the Middle West—an itinerant independent street teacher, a hobo
on the Ohio preaching the gospel of protest and abstinence—across
to the shore and finally down to Texas, now here in Xyn, a shelter
from taxes.

This god spoken of, within this territory, seemed but one of a billion
starring in this nation's stories. A poet by unpaid profession, a skeptic
by free confession, I had cast doubts on any host's or intercessor's
or ghostly blesser's ability to save a man's, a woman's, a child's,
a community's, a soil's soul. I came here to investigate and,
after meeting David, prostrated, babbling my testament to the pavement:
Waycross' streets to Xyn are the roads to roam!

And what was so telling (if you can stir it less turgidly)?

The way, without spelling, he could tell my nature and embrace me
as a lost son, not as a point to be used in pleadings and proceedings,
to be tossed back to feed the weeds, with unfulfilled needs,
after the first party has succeeded.

It was a conversion without conversation.
With no queries for the weary,
they took a tramp off the street, cleaned me up, fed me, bed me,
leaving me wondering, "When's the wedding?"

Tramping? Jumping from a grass bed to a bed-hopper?
Who in the Family counseled you for reform?

Not beds. Rail cars. For a while, I haven't been concerned about sacking
any land, female, or male—only a hearty meal. There were no suggestions
of reform. Actually instead, as this position shows, it was requested
that I perform. In other venues, I'm virtually a virgin.
Like you
. . . right?

(Pig, gorging at the trough of unscrumptious presumptions.)

I'm saving myself for one who saves me.

That's what we and the Father love to hear!

(No one reforms a trash-mouth, a shifty drifter,
but here I'm still treated as a careless one's sweepings,
brushed under a cut rug!)

So, what's to be believed of David?

I'm not so much into serving beliefs as I am into observing
and absorbing, understanding and then releasing. What do you use
to weave and move you through what is known and what is feared?

If a belief works, it's true;
If it fails, it's false.

Simple.

Well, you seem to be in complicity with the simplicity.

Oh no no no, I wasn't implying "simple-mindedness."

The truth is that which is verifiable by experience;
that which is "real" is that which is useful.

Um . . . How about we move on?
As a sunrise-surmise, I guess you, like me and some of your
formerly-vagabond Siblings in the Family, were a waif, only you
probably weren't forced to flee from wife-threatening strife.

Oh no? Say that kindly after I relate the details of the divorce.

I fled from two who were wed "out of duty"—an opening scene
for a production staged for the godly community
who reputedly saved them, and, by accepting, disposed of their sins.
Revamping the story of the two who produced me, cutting the cord
and dumping their unscrubbed, chubby, grubby lump
into the scumtub of history to rot until forgotten.

But you were adopted . . . ?

I was captured; raptured by the State,
brought back down to earth by Fate;
used as a symbol by the insane to prove to the weird world
they could maintain a normal, healthy family, progressing
ever further away from their incandescent, post-pubescent
transgressions against morality.

Out in public, they smiled, quietly—it was their fundamental duty.
At home, before or after my dish of corporal punishment, screams
and verbal riots ran to and about me. They weren't into receiving,
let alone believing, anything I had to give;
so they inspired me to leave.

Your guardians?

The Children.

Your friends?

Mostly unknowns.

One fey day at school was marked as my final
by the slaying of twenty-four classmates
by a chortling couple of others. I was to be
the twenty-fifth, but I was reprieved—again rescued
in a rapture
by the State's agents.

From that day on, a chorus of twenty-four silent voices
has inspired me to discover my Self and, then, my own
"road to roam" with lyrics and humming,
chants mimicking drumming,
vocal-step stammering and hammering.
I follow their council above that of others.

Uh-huh. From where are these sounds coming?

Their bodies have perished but their spirits reside in my head.
In my younger days, I was forced to be a singer.
Now I am simply a voice of silence.

Hmm . . . Resting unsplintered into "interesting."
Far from saviors, this State's agents contributed
to the death of my neighbors.

Snorting or squealing, they put their hooved prints on our land,
covered terrible territory with strange stories, turning cousin
against brother, friend against sister, then snuck out
like white silent winds. They watched from afar as two camps emerged,
hollering for war. The chaperons of this nation papered the wallflowers
of both sides as they committed calculated fratricide by dozing and
tipping cows, bulldozing, demolishing my neutral friends' houses
so they couldn't be used as quarters or resources for the other side.

Finally,
when one side opted to cop out of the welfare-warfare arrangement,
this nation's patriotic patriarchs, in collusion, stepped up support
for the other side. More than money, weapons and bodies
were provided in a one-sided war of confusion over nothing more
than three telephone poles.

After the flow of guns and funds was stanched, the blood kept on going,
Promising to blanch the souls of any who remained. And to insure
the flood, sanctions were imposed on my homeland by this houseland.
Food, medicine, and vital supplies couldn't come into the country,
but thousands of its children's lives left the Earth each year.

I was a hands-down, hands-on architect, reduced to stealing and killing
to save the lives within my family. Violence: the resource of the powerful,
the recourse of the powerless.

We held our own for a while, but apparently there was one more powerful:
My house was bombed. Only I survived. I viewed it as God's retribution
and attribute that event with pushing me to and with the currents of
the dead pool of pacifism. I soon after came here to find political allies
to cleanse the country of hypocrisy and the grime of other moral crimes.

Homeless there. Homeless here.

Until I could find a house, a family, and a home to build.

And the war back there?

It still wages, filling pages.
O, the fascination we all hold for fascist nations!
All praise the people who try to fulfill their obligations to their nation,
never mind the station in which the State put them.

And you came here to help your country
by eating out of cans and sleeping on streets?

. . . . . This session isn't about me.

Then that begs the question, if you'll pardon the expression: How am I
to be helped by us exchanging sad stories without endings? You are
to preach to me? About what? Cowardice? Base opportunity-seeking?

Hold on.
I wasn't homeless because I'm careless,
but because I care too much.

(Ugh.
Should I shoulder the burden of these tired, lazy, shiftless,
unexcused words?)

Nowhere will I slave for wages that'll be scalped to fund the anti-poor,
war-waging machine of bureaucratic bandits.

I wasn't on the streets selling hats and the tricks that come under them
as accessories. My crimes were more perverse: creating protest art,
passing out
subversive poetry.

And what was that to accomplish?
Hoping to get your work published?

Hoping to rope a streetwalker with a muddy heart and rocky power
to make vocal my rhymes, inspiring action in the name of the law
against a rapacious, infanticidal State.

Sun critics quip and query: "Where is the pure poem
composed by the premiere poet?" I reply at night: "Grip tight.
I have yet to have written it."

Shariah, I'm not a man of the cloth; neither overdressed nor nude.
You've more than potential—you've exercised, been chosen—
but you've an unexorcised gritty attitude.

David has been watching you in confinement and has passed his list
of refinement wishes on to me. Following the letter of catechization,
trying to ascertain with acumen, I sense you get anxious in the presence
of possible disease. Knowing where I came from
(from the base of a germ-inscribed obelisk
to top the totem pole of vermin)
must be uncomfortable for you; and knowing something of your origin,
I can guess no less than why. David says you're a compulsive neatnik.
None of us can be wholly pristine unless we retrace our unholy steps . . .

Look, don't even try to tell me I should flee back to the suspiciously specious
holey aegis of my legal guardians, into arms unwilling and unable, and
the commandments of their hosts, the watchful community.

You fled from your birthing country
when they most needed your help in rebuilding.
Your parents cared for your presence;
mine despaired over mine.

Stop being so offensively defensive and listen . . .
Let's not split a peaceful counseling session into two one-person
councils of aggression. I want to help you reconcile with your self,
all the while holding your hand, endearing my heart to help you
in this endeavor to pass from fire through smoke to a white cool light.
Mewling in the termite-infested pews, you sing your background
as a mere tragedy, but I see pure poetry—pyro-technique: Burn the flesh
to get to the soul, the depth of the truth, freeing both as one.
The trick is to do this under a desert moon—not with a torch
at high noon.

Now, the howling . . . . .
peyote?

No.

Tripped down by rocks,
stuck up in cracks?

Cocaine?

Yes.

No.
Sleeping with Mary Jane.

Yeah; and her maiden name is cocaine.
Alternating puffs and stuffs while milking, mooing,
mewing, rolling in sparring and purring conniptions.
What tender lessons does she impart
while using your brain cells
for your heart's tinder?

Fussy hussy, she's not—
waiting in white patience as her patient drops
some grab-enticing flab. If I should ever desire to acquire,
the Children, spurring, spin the wheel, incurring.

Spin it in a minute. We'll see in three.
The Children led you here for further instruction, right?

If they wanted me to stop smoking, they would've told me.

They led you to me. I'm telling you.
You're going to fall off, come to—
Wait and watch before attempting to strike a match.
I'm only four squared.

And I'm but one square more.
So, to tell, I know—
Hypocrisy, well.
Your sandals are made of cannabis.

I'm not smoking them.

But, having previously stepped on many jagged rocks, your foot is now
in your mouth, and a flame is traveling up
from a region down south.

While on this land, it's either this footwear or barefoot.
I won't be constricted, tied down with laces or strapped, stripped,
restricted from my initial identity. I wear these sandals
because they're the only footwear I can assemble on my own.
As far as the material, it's the best I had access to at the time;
plus, it's interwoven. I purchase little and make much,
all in an effort to starve the gluttonous machine
with an inhuman digestive system.

You have no sincere thoughts on the war at home.

You have but sinful feelings of love for self and others,
a love dubbed as "loathing,"
ranking more appropriately with rancor.

My effort for the war today is to sabotage the machinery
of the factories, with their grand soul-releasers, smoke-stacks, wide doors
taking in human bodies as light snacks; never starving, never having
too much to munch on. Cut the candleless pie, carve out an end to this
industrial age.

As for ours, twenty-five may be the wise end to adage
to those on the course who are nine behind—but it's not the right number
for a children's chorus. How can your keen sense allow you to continue
to drive such a cancerous career, knowing each time you turn to ignite,
you might reverse the right saga that left you a survivor?

What compels me? Whining whims based on the education
of experience. Can't stay stagnant in repose, or power posing
as interminable will surely die, the power to connect with unseen
souls and convey their energy. To continue moving, evolving,
progressing is essential to living.

And the nation of destiny? You obviously prefer oblivion.

Some emotions are true fuel,
but many—siphoned to feed the feud of possibilities—
are too cruel for the sensibilities.
Emotions mixed with memories become potions which,
when consumed, imbibed, drunk,
cause physical disabilities.

(Her own wonkish wiles are monkishly beguiled. Apparently
she doesn't wear all this loose clothing for modesty, but due to her
losing the shame game. Her own image in her eyes lies, adding mounds,
pounds, and unfounded suspicions. Her heightened self-consciousness
has grown to extra-consciousness, causing her to groan and mount
an assault against any fault, no matter how minute, pinpointed
in the appearance
and actions of others.)

Abducted by lawless aliens, you may ransom your own wisdom, dear.
Nearer to you is a wealthy entity, the very abductor
of your reasoned sanity. These are our Times of Compassion;
you've highlighted my sandals,
but I see your moccasins.

Though automatic minutes and seconds tic clocks, pushing us
nearer the wall of our first session, I've settled on a mutual therapy
—an aloe vera massage for the mentality. Nothing cosmetic,
but a detoxification method that, if done correctly, will mush and push us
to savor original thoughts served with the sauce of the cosmos.

Instead of permitting them to abuse, stew and use those memories
to feed new artistic theories that'll help repair a system, rebuild
a strong body, and then exercise until your pores inspire the unnamed
animate rejects and inanimate objects within the viper radius of your
inner sourced, solar-sweetened, vaporizing perspiration.

Enriched ideas—if solid, probably too much to munch on.
Your elaborate verbal manna and rain dance seems to have produced
an abundance of ghosts instead. Ironic: Despite your oxymoronic
verbal tonic, I'm parched. Cinch the clouds and quench
my lack of understanding.

Driving a syllabus for transportation, I propose for our next session
we tap into the source of what has scared some sacred. We'll begin
the amusing maze, at the end of which is an orb to be absorbed, entered
into the center.

To you in whom David places unadulterated trust, wisdom, instructor:
Come out of your sitting fort, if you're able to stand comfortably,
and give me the real dead deal.

Just adjust and equal
some sense
a little less dense!

Art.
I'm a verbalist.
You're a songstress (maybe my voluptuous muse materialized).
I can compose lyrics for you to sing that'll help you see
to the very core of your being—subconscious self-reforming process
from the inside out. You'll find herbs deep in the vowels of verbs.
We can practice the next hour.
And, soon, in the Family room.

I forgot to be loud about my inability to sing in front of crowds—
It's a vow made upon maturity, trying to scour scores of sores,
security against inciting snapping sounds,
reopening young wounds,
exciting impurities.

Switches. The knocks of familial knots at the end of taut lines clipped,
reared, and whipped—in your position of confinement, I see how it
may be an imposition to feign refinement and give an anxious answer.

But though, as an admonishment, it may seem caustic, the effect
of the cause will astonish, refresh; I promise. You can't away
from a familial famine into a feast
without preparation.

After the wild, there are spoils of war,
sparing of the rod, and spoiling of the child.

That's supposed to be an incentive?

It's proposed as an invective.
As the child goes on, it is spoiled as neglected food is—
wasted, nourishing none, but possibly poisoning many.

I was never spoiled!

You want to be so here.

I'm not an entertainer.

Neither am I;
just an initiate who becomes intimate with that which intimidates
in order to make it all plainer.

(Riding ridiculous riddles on the low edge of knowledge,
under the dumb dome of wisdom.)

Embattled and embittered by the self-inflicted welts
from conflicted belts, I recognize the truism that the altruistic artist
can calm qualms at their varied sources
as well as
throughout the Multiverse.

Use your competitive competence,
submit to the temporary temptation,
ignore the tempter, forget the temperature,
meticulously pursue, and immaculately subdue . . .

now, what do the Children tell you?

I . . .
I can't sing with
. . . these cheeks.
A chipmunk just chews.

Choose to produce a dynamic testimony.
In the maze: Refrain from the thin lines,
ascertain and contour your path by touching pulse to impulse.
Dwell in this well: It's not what the artist intends,
but what the audience extracts.

Well, someone in the audience may say one thing,
think another, and act
in accordance
with a third way.

Though hate hits hard, often,
know: Love, soft, is gloved.

The message: After all boxing battles,
those involved are due for a tender massage.

". . . wouldn't even condemn this until it scaled to proportions epidemic
or it was discovered for them that their own mothers were once daughters.
Slap the ambivalent powers with empathy.
Some swift raps of adjectives might make the groaning inept into apt pupils.
The formerly self-absorbed may grow into rapt supporters for the recapture.

"Maybe some will heed requests, be in attendance
next Wednesday for our special speaker—a survivor, an escapee.
She'll appear to give insight, relating the lurid episodes of her own life—
kidnapped, trapped in a trailer, an unwitting assistant of terrorists
in activities sexual, brutal, fatal—all criminal.

"For any who failed in filial obligations and extras, or sought to curtail,
to no avail, the eruption of insolence in innocents, the erection of inviolate
barriers from parents; for those whose attempts at comfort were translated
into confrontations, which inevitably escalated;

"support our group, Children in Arms (CIA), a mechanistic mission
that seeks to reclaim gullible, juvenile runaways from the multifariously
nefarious attractive traps outside the familiar, socialize them within
the proper sanctuaries, adhering to the politics of relationships.

"Currently, our membership is comprised of concerned and victimized
parents, social workers, cult deprogrammers, and retired bounty hunters.
A nonprofit enterprise dedicated to healing the sores
of vile lives and evil loves.
Please join us next week.
Hors d'oeuvres will be served."

JIHAD AND RUMORS OF PEACE

"You have immortal abilities beyond claymen's ken,
                                according to the Word,"
David said. "God scripted your name to yours truly,
each line of each letter of which was a kenning.
Rendered tender: You're a poet, one who constructs
                                new realities with terms.

"As this is the case, I want you to undertake a mediating mission
akin to but estranged from your regular sessions."

An old cold war to warm a welcome in my new home.
Wonderful. Mystics versus philosophers.
David won't stand calm to see God's Family witness against itself.

Chosen for talent alone? I'm not prone to believe so
as David has admitted he admires my stance on authority:
A secure, higher Justice should be the managing editor
over secular, earthly authoritarians.

Lack of Love and respect reigns
with canonites firing cannonballed phrases,
bibliophobes harping on bibliophiles;
it's disconcerting that it's come up to this now.

The Family's mystics dance too much, dwell little,
try to repeat the feats on water surfaces.
The soft philosophers seem less loyal, royal-stalling,
                                thinking themselves into stone.

David wants intelligent enthusiasts.
And yet how can I be any less of a moral model?
My thoughts within will dwell upon Shariah,
                                and the dovish laws of Love.

Settled:
since this Sabbath sermon will interfere
with my scheduled one-on-one with Shariah,

during which I was planning to offer her a proposal,
I'll simply hitch the two.

CALL TO ARMS

I know a little about a lot,
this lot we call our "families."
So knowing, David requested I cap the Sabbath sermon
with a display of sound, heralding a time for hugs and handshakes.

Said David, to aid my conversion,
I must produce a truce during a maelstrom
to repent for running from home
(using smoke and flames for diversion).

God, save me!

He heard my wails of travails and revealed himself
as a musician. He'll pick the strings during my presentation,
picking their heads free of tangles, sticking together split ends—
". . . to make the body know they're crucial to making the head beautiful."

His analogy deserves apology.
A young woman, yes; but I care for more than hair.
I've never fashioned myself as a prophetess,
but livid I'm considered so lucidly vapid.
Perhaps God should be enlightened.

Children, make me translucent!

I've lived a life in a different cult where I was
challenged to undertake tasks no less
difficult than solving the combinations
of Love and slavery only so others might profit.

Thanks, God, for your permission to pontificate,
prophesy to your proselytes and acolytes alike.
Sure, I'll mend the muslin curtains rent by the claws and beaks
of harpies and chirpies; I'll share an experience,
exhort them to listen to seditious traditions,
but not to let those dictate.

So shield your eyes lest they be thread with these lights:
a life of plight, glorious retrievals, unholy assumptions,
and insanely rational rights.

TWISTER
(Hanid's Lesson)

Creation—an informal education
for the initiated to engage in meditation.
I came here as you, to hone my skills
as a mediator for His lesser creatures.

Read nature's blessed lessons, penetrate the veil.
Divine law twists like serpents eating their own tails.
Sunny cyclone—heed my tone, but fear nothing.
Sunbursting tears are Love's features.

Experience what so often frightens,
            enlightens those readied for knowing:
Glowing words spinning off new worlds,
            hurled off in pairs—seen and unseen,
green and blue—accompanied by a freight train
            rain noise; twister of sunrays;
days of bright floods! What's more beautiful,
            dutiful than male and female sharing Intelligence?

God's direction—a rotation, falling and rising.
We've a duty to imitate, passionately baptizing
our minds in the funneling Spirit. Hear It!
I've encountered a child of Love nearing nova!

            Interactions have been somewhat frequent;
delinquent at times, I was apprehensive,
            pensive too much; such enlightening flees
free from philosophy's camps of concentration.
            Contemplation, mystic, retrieves the distant,
constant in their search for holy fire's power.
            Flowers grow in the soil of the soul's bed
fed by the drops that follow the star's contractions.

            Trust: Our vacuum attracts more than God's lost dust.
            Armies are arming to come kill our Father, scatter us!

Our duty is to attain divinity!
Divinity equals divine unity.

Smokers of reason on your cool mountains,
     fountains in your warm valleys, as one
come to the middle plains—thinkers, tinkers,
     drinkers of the ecstasy! Lightning and loud thunder
wonders will accompany the celebration,
     culmination, in our body's mind, of peace!
Decreased its appearances out there—Love's Spirit.
     It was feared, unwanted here among God's brokers.

THE NEW AGE OF REASON
(Shariah's Lesson)

Elementary learning experience:
My sense of Presence, from where did it come?
In the Spirit, mystifying sensations,
presentations of God's Nature to one.

Your stature is irrelevant, audience;
Love blew a kiss to one sun,
the reaction spun

moist air, manifold halos, spiraling
splendor of indigo, green, red bands.
Despite the bright delight, the torrents terrify some
who mistake our life-turning quest as a march to burn.

Blue calm in my eye belies the process of maturation, accelerated:
Going deeper within, centering, to find Truth, the pressure level
                                        is lowered low,
pushing outward; your eyes are opened to a suffering society.
But, once Love's found within, you release

a bountiful array of yellow, violet spray:
Frozen Love melted by holy fire.
Visual lyrics dousing all surrounding,
arousing passions for submission to the Beautiful.

Usher in this New Age of Reason:
A philosopher-poet will set the Multiverse
with diverse seasons, rationing more than four
to satisfy the brain-numbed hungry, sore-thumbed thirsty.

The supreme charity is Love's clarity.

THE RULES OF ENGAGEMENT

I should have more to divulge, but I'm spent.

What's this essence you enfold in issues during every sermon
when you raise semantic flags, spangled with tangible angles, for me?

Take out "more," you'll be less likely to mislead other listeners.
Skies have eyes, airs have ears—so I sustain the stained speech.
On this eve, I wish the positions switched, at least once.

Attempting a coup?
Attempting a couple
in order to accord due Love.
Let's reverse the roles, with me in a malaise,
you as impressional master, freeing Love ensconced.

I have to leave . . .
You've left, and returned to a time to examine yourself,
one luminous patient.
You think my body that free for visions to enter?

Why take such affront, push back one enamored?

Some who are so unkind to our kind
propose mercy marriages to enshrine, flash Love blind,
knowing none wholesome would deign to entertain
that one so blemished could see true Love.

Experience is tenured but still only a teacher in one area.
You came seeking redemption. Although I'm the son of liaisons,
I'm untutored in the rules of engagement.

Aren't all your songs a call for men to comprehend?
I'm seeking to further our edification.
The small voices inside you have cried for my answer.

One lesson on Love: Bury it, it is preserved in this world;
                    burn it, it is reserved for the next.
The Children urge me to give their reply in vows

woven with the threads used for your flags.
Tomorrow night, in a quarantined seminar,
> *I'll pass on another secret, numinous teaching . . .*

TRINITY POLYGAMY

Resilience is an attribute I can easily claim proudly;
it's the plump, dumpy semblance with which I'm not pretty-pleased.

Secrets in the core of Omniscience—
What did God's Messenger find so beauteous?

Better instead that I repent for committing coital crimes of compassion.
Feel sorry? I felt sorry; that's why I did it.
Question again: Is it sin if consensual?
But David,
          when he saw me look askance, rushed to hush with a revelation.

He knows all that transpires within his vicinity.
He will forget, forgive if I submit fully to his will.
David is inspired, instructed by sketches
drawn in his head by the hand, the fingers of God.
Last night, a masterpiece was created. Meditated, communicated:
God, in the person of David, is to wed immediately
the current incarnation of the Holy Spirit, known now as "Shariah."

Together, we're to produce the anointed Redeemer.
Hanid is important, but only as a presage.
Hostage captured in a picture, host to the New Age of Reason . . .
but what section will I bring in?

"I lie by the Truth" was his parting phrase that hour.
He's a mystery most to those who know him best;
less a cosmic perfection, more like a comic to those who know the least.
Dare I defy one with the power to deify?

Crimes of compassion, come pass again:
two husbands: one taken to soothe a soul that suffered in the past,
the other taken to soothe the souls of countless millions that will suffer
if this promised Pacifier is not born to give.

Can I intentionally conspire with the molesters
                                        or murderers of Roy G. Biv?
Star quality of mine, come to play your role.

Placid sipper of the ethereal, still I'm inclined to say:
"God, go away. Love, leave me to fall into the romance of ignorance.
To hell, condemn them all!"

Take three breaths, gather your composure . . .
rather, prepare for the rapture—
an Omnipotent Being wants to be with me!

The veins of vanity are suddenly flowing with life!
Perhaps my unarresting looks aren't crooked cops thieving gaiety from me
but a paradoxed box of a blessing not to be questioned,
like my God's mystery.

EXTRACT FROM A RELIGIOUS
ORGANIZATION'S NEWSLETTER

". . . proliferation of sects vying for dominance, vying for independence
in the western part of our Nation, most with nefarious intentions.

"In this issue, we focus on one, infamous, right in the next county:
The Xynites, long a broken branch of religion
housed at the Mound Xyn Center, known as 'The Anthill.'

"Members, remember: All sects secularize, resulting in cults
who praise and attempt to raise over God
one worldly nature: the carnal.

"The Xynites recognize as their Mother-Father one failed rock-and-roll
musician, androgynous in appearance: David X, a charismatic charlatan
who believes in the immortality of his own immorality.

"Cult experts suspect him as a pedophile, expect him to turn rapist.
He fits the virile profile based on the word of undisciplined disciples
who, infuriated by the depraved ravings of Dave and the prominence
of promiscuity, emerged from an emergency of anti-Body debauchery.

"They've relayed to us that The Anthill houses breeders whose sole
purpose is to produce infants, selling them for thousands
south of the border.

"Let us pool our power with Concerned Religious Relatives,
a mainstream group whose members have lost blood to this cult
of prostitutes, addicts, perverts, and lights for baby traffic.

"Let us incite others to fight with a campaign of wrought letters; excite,
write to politicians and editors, providing insights on the rattling battles
of those who have fought to prevent a pregnant problem from regenerating
until regnant.

"To stifle paralyzing debate, let us push for a temporary unification
                                                        of temple
                                                    and State.

Pest control of red devil ants (deviants of the Fire)

rests under temporal authority
influenced by the Truth, which lies with the orthodox, the majority."

64

SOLOMON'S SEAL

After a week of seeking and failing to find steady work for wages
to help me pull my own weight with my Family,
I traveled back into Waycross, that soulful weighing station,
on Saturday afternoon for recreation.

I decided to take in a play with a theme
                                    seeming profanely mundane—
my mind needed a respite from the whirls of the weird world.

No avail. The uncurtailed gusts of wailing gales entered through
several of my body's nine gates. The props, tones, and notes
were to most, surely, arcane, but to me
                                    the propaganda was so strained.

When the curtains fell, I felt pity for those who walked away
complaining or merely entertained, knowing nothing
unexplained.

The somber play, DAVID AND LEVIATHAN,
was about a twisted sect leader who hides his actions
behind simple perversions of popular perceptions
                                    of a complex law.
The backstory claims to be based on authentic events.

So impressed with the inducing tale of shucksters and hucksters, I
snuck backstage to meet the Impresario and suggest a mutual production
for the future.

Solomon, the playwright, was a sullen fellow, but hardly dull.
In truth, he brightened when told of the original land, crescent,
from where I hailed. His wife's of foreign extraction and,
at a crucial time, provided an enriching distraction
from a pinching attraction.

We went on to discuss his disgust at the role
concerned citizens' censor boards had played
in getting his play banned in certain sections
of the country.

"It's all because," he said in his own words,
"I'm an incendiary visionary."

So he's forced to play to tiny theatres
in unknown towns.

An opening: I welcomed him and his troupe outside of town
to play at the Mound Xyn Center, if only we may combine
our talents in a mission in the near future.

He didn't appreciate the wedding invitation.

After an unbalancing silence, he warned his next words would depreciate
that value I held on David and his Family, both doomed by the massive
monster of the sea of masses, the one portrayed in the play.

A play of augury written by one former member of the Family
who went on to reveal the history behind events to come:

"David's a charlatan who fell from the Midwest,
the Love Child of a careless carpenter and child abuser
who soon left his wife—a virgin of twice seven years—alone, again.
David was repeatedly raped as a child, growing.
He dropped out of school to divorce theories and embrace realities,
but before doing so, he acquired facts to know
'As it is above, so so below.'

             "So, as in the beginning . . .

"David is now the carpenter who constructs shoddy,
                                        unstable structures
using materials, fatigued and fragile.

"All the women of the Family are eventually married
into the harmonious harem
of David's House while the men are to be sexless, joyful,
celibate workers toiling on his buildings and their stories
to shield his violations from the public.

"Guessing his fetish due to incredibly bad credit,

Harmony's Harem counts as members, primarily, pre-married women;
of those that are unmarried, they are pre-pubescent.

"Such pungent deeds for fertilizing one's seeds must be sanitized,
washed clean.

"Although there is precedent,
it's dubious that all David's Family traditions
derive from a source higher than that of the Nubians.

"I left shouting running comments, no longer able to rightly stand
as everyone silently bowed to fulfill his uncommon commands.

"David was once truly inspired, about the time I came in.
But staying a course of stubbornness, he refused to swerve when
God begged him; he began listening to his own notes, not the Lord's.

"It's written: If any rivals to God's authority are set up on the Earth,
the subjected Leviathan shall arise to consume, reclaim."

Sol's prophecy in his play insists the worldly authorities
                                        will soon get involved
and bring authentic justice to the statutory rapist
—if that's what David truly is.

"That's why I stage such plays
—to raise the public's righteous consciousness."

After a stabilizing silence, I quoted some appropriate original verse.
Decrypting my encryptions, he delivered a phrase in a reversed hearse.
Then, smiling, he drove and parked this carriage:
            "Are you married to your occupation?
                    Preoccupied, groom, with your doomed marriage?"

If not, I could feel free to join him in employment of an enjoyment.
His troupe had been looking for a proficient poet to aid, in deed;
but true poetry, in his eye, requires surgery.
"Not the cosmetic kind, mind you,
but that which does not flatter ghosts
as it seeks to save lives first and foremost."

Privileged, I accepted and he took and told me in confidence about David:
"I hate him with a passion unknown to mortal men."
As if I couldn't conjecture as much from the play bolstered by the lecture.

For our collaboration on one man's sin,
an artistic spin—insider looking out; outsider looking in.
Our goal: To bring an updated version of DAVID AND LEVIATHAN
to a popular stage for a worldwide audience.

FOR THE CRESCENT TO CROSS THE STAR

First, a gob of God, released and falling,
                              created all through a resounding yell
as it fell. Predestined, bound for earth,
                              which it created through sound,
the gob took human form upon its landing,
plucking itself from its own muck and mire.
Mixing elements from both origins,
it established an empire on a solid rock.

Act one.
First draft.
A silent wind befriends,
          inspiring a prayer of fire:

          Give me strength
          to turn exorcist, drown out songs the hardy fear to hear,
          lead an exodus of kin who see selling sex for a prophet is sin, queer,
          suck on a lemon, pucker up and whistle a kiss,
          signaling enemies on my page to engage others on the list.
          Free for all:
          Giant squid governments with vast, sucker-bearing arms,
          two of ten with tentacles that seize and bring innocents to harm,
          versus equally corrupt religion, organized, bread-fed
                              into a behemoth.
          I vow now to lift my life to disrupt the wars of both.

Act two:
This earthbound god divided his empire (singing the singular into plural)
then demoted himself from ruler to a mere counselor,
promising to self not to meddle in human affairs . . .
until he took a virgin from among them against her will.
Sparked a battle to kill her husband, blew into infernal wars
that continue to consume the world.

At this stage in the play,
          may they pray for eternal intermission . . .

God, reclaim
imperialists with freedom on lips, but swords of fire in hand,
moneymakers with no foundation on which they can,
                                        without tipping, stand,
intellects who teach nonsense with dusty books on their shelves,
and governments which rule with rules for everything
                                        but themselves.
Earth, reclaim
religions which preach God, but whose actions teach against Love,
tax collectors with death in eyes and axes in glove,
mindless ants with no business who do their best to mind mine,
and rapists who take from life, viewing their finds as fines.

To the audience, the question to ponder:
        Where do creators, even rulers,
                acquire the power to measure, straighten,
                        destroy the lives of all under?

                                We give them ours.

Earth, reclaim
the life of this world and all its rushed vain pursuits,
the small children who gasp and grasp for titles and suits,
all acts of apathy coupled with sitting complaints,
and empty discourse that holds the conscience in restraint.
God, reclaim
the business of selling salt to those who have thirst,
the endless games of blind men who put appearances first,
and those who fight to die for the State's cult with jealous zeal.
Pig's weal—
How far will the squeal carry beyond the silence
                                of Sol's seventh seal?

PART III:
THE DESCENT
AND SCALE

THE ANTHILL

. . . . . There is a word for what happened then:
In the rich much later of a struggling power outage (a god's storm)—
the old headmaster long ago expelled
from around the holes of worms abandoned,

dilapidated clapboard cottages snapped apart,
demolished hovels unshoveled—

the body had to be modeled again.

Rays on Monday, she awakens with miniscule granules clogging
every flogged pore of her exodermis. Orange-thirsty for first breakfast
for peace, but the debris' hubris pushes the grits to the lips and tip and
buds of her tongue. Over there, up under the sun, a trade-parade, works
on premises without promises, has begun. Barking, they'd razed a village
to raise a barn; pieces of cracked, broken vessels huff and snuff
seeking to save the burning sparks. Landslide from the outside in,
down the trachea. Choke on the chores while asking the task . . .

One mature maternal world, her echo-system breached; face sacrificed;
rosy cheeks, bleached; nocent stubble on every inch of skin; rubble
sliding, caking, devastating within. Imagine windmills to save them:
kith and kin; laborers, friends and neighbors: raspily lung-sung,
the nascent ants march forth from the gular pith to work the gravid
graveyard shift (morning star has fallen). For end's benefit, they
pretend the gummy crumbs they assist up, out of the mouth
went down the windpipe
by accident.

Mellifluously, the eclecticists (blacks, browns, yellows, and reds)
evacuate the cavity, backtracking along the ecliptic. Launching wide
away from the chin, one with the Multiverse, the Trojans hurry-scurry
to toil upon the evocative barren prairie, ditching, switching, stitching,
spicing the dermis, readying the body for its return to, through space.
Precise excavations; diligent servants will stick with one
through thick skulls
and thin skins.

Her unique gastronomical passion (unceasingly rebirthing the earth,
the seas) may one day induce the loose screws to scrutinize, re-critique

their fellows in an astronomical fashion. Envisioning forty-one storied
residential edifices dotting the marbled third egg, all oriented to face,
in meditation, the reconstructed Ranch Revelation.

Till when: On the next spot, a sudden gush from a hidden vent
in her healing ecosystem venerates, hoisting a bonnet,
                                        a headdress,
                                            a moist flag:
A large star encircled by a serpent skinned with twelve others, lesser.

BESIDE BEDSIDE MANNERS

By noon on a Tuesday, none had witnessed our god,
long overdue at his podium to arrest, push us into fitness
by asserting his opinions. Worried witless, burping opportunists
convoked a cafeteria gathering, tuning their harps with conspiracy fears,
theories, and more than a countable number of queries.

Suffering for automatic minutes, spin seconds, toc tic,
on the hot air debates on the politics of relationships, quietly, I rose
as a solo man and took a can of alphabet soup, a bowl, and utensils,
and headed upstairs. Conscience kicked by the spurious and the curious,
I went under the cloud of dusty pretense to aid an undoubtedly sick man.

With a poor knocking, I opened the door, entering the pen
of the quarantined; hidden pencil with invisible lead ready to note
the expected abhorrent deeds of the aberrant white silhouette . . .
still in his pod, under sheets, alone, bearing a sharp smile.

After an embarrassed silence,
I attempted to gloss my faux pas with some excuse
about coming to equip the famished gypsy west of Egypt
so he may continue his trip south for the day's sermon.

Soreless, he thanked me for answering his psychic summons.
There would be no preachy teachings today, he said, only a "man-to-man,
arm-to-hand, each-to-each." He rose to close the shades, asked me to abet
by getting the door. Abed again, me sitting at his side, he confided in me
—infidelity with the infidel.

He has a "Grand Plan for the Planet"—a repopulation program that,
under free light, is despicably rascally. He invited me to be
(in my words, a staunch protector of the raunch, stanching the prying sight
of outsiders around the ranch), in his words,
                              his thirteenth letter times three:
his "Mighty Mystery Man," responsible for shielding his "glory"
from those who make up stories. Knowing the substance, I'm the man
to guard the secret of the Plan
                    with the pistol he took from under his pillow
and thrust into my hand.

Irresponsive, despondent thanks to his irresponsibility
at having firearms within the reach of so many, some kids. This bastard
continued to amend two of the tenets of his Demandments. Presuming
one conferred with such an honor as mine
would be pumped up with pomposity, caring nothing for pity,
my complementing duty would be to embrace the self-intimacy
of semi-celibacy—temporarily,
until married to the Spirit in heaven.

Although his appalling yin and appealing yang were initially taken
with a grain, Solomon's seals truly reveal, make plain.

       Pencil sharpened . . .

SHEKINAH

For the lost profound world and unseen reality to be,
his compulsory effacing sacrifice is to be chastised physically
—with ulcers, fevers, colds, and spinal throes—for the transgressions
possessed by the Family.

Carefully vicarious: to temptations, succumbed; three sucked thumbs;
unmeasured pleasures are to be his experience,
while they indulge in fervent abstinence.

Fostered reprobance. Upbraidings liquefied.
Obscenities' clarity:
In the bunk, we lie
as the miser takes his misery from me.
"Loving in vain is to leave God in pain" . . .
so I'm learning at an expense. Lying
with any besides him is adultery, the epitome
of sins.

Iniquity imposed on me by the one who takes tap-miss pains
to gain sympathy for himself in order to exploit his Way. Disposable;
away with my virginity. Without inquisition, David proposes to me
a chance to acquire equality (the first person in life to offer her
an advantage); in addition, he'll commute the Panderer's position,
naturally expanding my commission.

Unwitting phenomenon: Heading down to the end of rationality's road;
it could only take me out so far. Now an eccentric trout, I fin the stream
leading to fantasies' times' seas. Reloading the melody: Basis of a bias
on Sibling selects: David's music in garish performances
                          accented with a dash of hyper-typical artists
opens the portals between sealed realities
and ascending mortals.

David desires a band, traveling, to spread the bread
and gather new preservers,
with me as the buttery lead singer,
unraveling the knits, settling the fits of dyspepsia.

From veracity through tenacity to sagacity,
we'll gig.

"First, you must diet:
refrain from singing with the pernicious Poet any longer.
His once delicious diatribes, contracting bacteria,
will soon be injurious.
You're eating for one tribe now."

Is the ordinary purpose of this to keep order
or give extraordinary directions?

"Stay reserved; revere your re-sent memories—
Witness that I, too, am watching my own figure."

True:
He suns in the tagging attention of clashed nutrition;
I'm to shun, shedding shier
under the gagging flashing of attrition.

"My mind and your soul for the goal of a glorious new body:
a definite trinity."

Funny: a body dimmed to slim only to glow voluminous again.
A recreated mortal desecrated; a morsel rejoined and excreted.
Past indiscretions: so illumined to almost feel, nauseate.
Hanid was my first. David is the real.
(Marriage born and show-known in its own initial consummation.)
The pervasive revolution with the evasive resolution:
Is He the Absolute effect or the Ultimate cause?

SPY TO THIEF

Composing black verse—convert a morose Morse—
asp back words: coded odes for the stage
placed on a grey public page, all born of white espionage

conducted, partially, in candid sessions
in which every gesture of the counseled is questioned.
Analysis of the pitter-patter of their chitter-chatter—
       There's platinum under banal conversations.

Once, I took in individuals' problems in confidence,
mulled and channeled therapeutic lessons to a wounded audience,
          after coloring to protect privacy, of course.
Now, I'm forced to sprinkle verbs of assault on my trusted friends,
beloved Siblings, until flat—rattle the scales already unbalanced;
use my tail talents to turn tattle-tales against the head.

Lunacy to attempt to protect both lives and privacy;
one must be given up. Clean percipients of peyote
so they may clearly survey the purveyor. Coyote

running on canvas-covered land, an overly fertile crescent,
to prevent a fall, must tirelessly chase tips, their scents.
Bound, my head may bob in clouds,
      but my feet are still planted in the ground.

Our Father in his haven, unshaven, is nothing
but a failed musician suffering from mania.
He split an "inner spirit" to console him,
claimed he found Truth and formed a union,
and established Xyn to direct Armageddon.

Originally hailing from Illinois,
he's still trying to keep a faithful band
and make them successful in famousing his name.

Although initially slow with an open mind,
I now have to move quickly to the day with my unblanketed convictions
since I've uncovered hearsay (heard said)

proof of his undoubtedly unwelcome clandestine relations
with a particular minor known only as his "orbiting spirit."

HEX

I sense an immense tension.

It's dissension
within you.
Kisses and other spatterings of saliva remunerated to me, a mere man,
while your full devotion's invested within a bag of fleas, a dog.

Oh? Have you investigated what you propagate?
Or is your paranoia ramming, running down the lanes of a panorama?

Tease what you please, but when your amorphous self grows old
into his mold, if your mind-brights aren't melded with his, your soul's heart
will melt when you become privy to the bureaucratic corruption.

Sniffing the winds ringing your rosy bush is exasperating!
Your medium is tedium . . .
Just hand me the hexagramic telegram you called me down here to receive.

Haven't you ever noticed, in spite of being enamored, how David
can provide much for many in the community, especially the children,
with just a part-time job as a small-town mechanic? Lumber, tools,
metal, meals, clothes, toys, bicycles, baby stuff—
So what's your dynamic?

Where does the primary income for this parish come from?

My guesses perish, this week's conspiracies too weak to speak.

Death-trading. Selling tools for killing, Frigid One. Guns.

Cowspit! That's obscenely absurd!

What? My words? Or his actions?
If it's the latter, I'll agree.
The former, we'll argue.

The fraudulent virtues, oil of vitriol
you're sprinkling on small David's tall character.

O my god! Gag reflex . . .
For a desperate, deliberate reader, you're so slow in mind
as to render your own critical vision blind! That jerkstick David,
while muttering some incoherence about "community economics"
and bolstering profit by acquiring and selling guns, handed me
this very pistol to protect him and his room while he tools
                    with little pretty nasties like you,
who once made the claim she hated guns! Now, you gorge—
Pit! Rot! Pure applesauce . . .
                    How can you say such malicious things to me?

I'm sorry.
I'm sorry . . . but this—
It was predicted to me. I knew David was a salacious
bleach-speeched greedy with a tall order of talent. Sol had said so,
in words more artistic, no less explicit.

"Saul"?
(Sounds like one foul soul.)

Yeah . . . "Sol." A former acolyte of David's, a member of Xyn's Family.
He was sagacious enough to leave when a spiritually immature father
started playing adultery. Now he has a blood-money scheme to sell guns
to help purchase food, clothing, shelter, and care "for the world's children"
. . . oh yeah, and to "spread the word." What the hell kind of care
can be bought or kept with guns involved? And exactly what types of words
are to be spread with such bawdiness and gaudily evil utensils?
                    What kind of god—
He never said he was "God"!

But that's his obvious purpose!
He wants us all to have full credentials of credulity.

Do you even believe in what you're trying to deceive with?

Believe? Growing in the groin; I know you're in an improper relationship.

And what is "proper"?

To admire what is True from afar; do what you think is right
and reject what is wrong, maintaining moral independence.

I seek a personal relationship, giving all to the Creator
in order to be cleansed and thus aid in the future Creation.

So I've seen.

You shouldn't mock what you don't understand.
Fear, while defective, is a more accurate response.

What about respect?
It's evident you don't understand my real feelings.

I'm not an entertainer. So I won't entertain
your unenthusiastic position notion, proposition
of prop devotion. I believe in Unseen Realities.

That's tantamount to saying, "I believe in the Future"
—what is undeniably in existence,
but what none in existence can see.

Most do deny, attempt to shield themselves from, or try to prevent
the Future from materializing. I know David. Unrelenting,
nonrepenting, he must, for our begin-sins, fall.

For what use will it be if fellows refuse to follow the law?
What example is he?
What sample are you?
How can you stand to sit around such clutter, such smut, such palpable
Filth in your particular teenage tilt?

My lilt guides me through, by, and away from steaming, bubbling sludge
such as that coming out of the mouth of you! The wrathful world is dying
in its waste of faith for wraiths,
lying in the unquestioned faith.

Ah, the tugging, hugging hex of sex
hung on the neck of one aged ten plus six!
Set the bait for dogs, what do you expect to catch?
But you don't want to confront. You want comfort.
Attract to a blue flame, wait till he's thoroughly fed
with a glossy coat
 and tame your god with games of fetch. But whose role is rolled?

Aren't you sing-bringing sticks, tricked,
back to him?

And who's writing my words of light?
You have no tact but you tacitly want a god that will follow you
in pants, retrieve your papers and reviews, and lick your face.
Or does your pal Saul have you in that four-legged place,
rear up?

We have come to serve a fishy egg, a caveat.

"We"?

You know the three: I, myself, and me.

(The insidious Enemies of Harmony.)

You and I need to take the next exit, detour from this sick soupy brothel
of impure righteousness. I swear it's due to truly become hell on earth,
an apocalypse to the world's watchers. No drenching downpour
from any rich sky's aqueduct will be adequate to quench
this waiting inferno.

And who'll be the arsonist, or the fire artist's son?

Are you thinking me?

I couldn't think any lower.
But I know between two, there's always a third.
So accusing would be useless . . .
Is it my time to whistle a reprise, negotiate a reprieve?

There'll be no alleviation, mollification, or mitigation.
The friends who received David's sins as gifts are waiting
for the next giving holiday season.

You're friends with such collusionists
who would face-off against David, his halo,
and his aura?

The phrase "my friends" wasn't chewed,
nor did it fall, flow, spit, or spew out of my mouth.

Yeah, but I know the laws of poetry:
                                       Unwritten rules that can't be spoken.
I'm including suspicions, but I love to be proven wrong.
It's the only way to learn.

Well, I'm inviting you to a class, one to conclude the rude one's run.
At his Sabbath sermon, I'm going to shoot god
                                with the very gun he gave me.
               There!
Equity without equivocation!

You have no chance.

Then I'll take a chance.

He offends by handing me a killing tool and pushing me to his front;
makes claims of my soul's defense by sleeping with my would-be wife
behind my back. Now you want me to give benefit back?
He'll have an attack.

I'm sure I'll be saving dozens, scores, or more.

The arrogance of heroics, exchangeable for innocence.
Acknowledge your intolerance of ignorance, acceptance of common sense.
This is no time to endanger yourself, him, me, or any in the community.
I've had a Spirit Experience . . .

                                    . . . I'm pregnant.

. . . . .
        I . . .
. . . . .
        Love . . .

(Being obsequious to my muse now is not a choice but a duty,
as is postponing David's inevitable obsequy.)

SALAM

*The celestial canopy split wide open
at midnight, dropping a golden ray of solid light,
then closed. The line to the source cut,
the ray fell, balled, rolled away, glittering
into the night.*

Six-hour-old miracle—living ore
freed to mature into an oracle—
contemplates her parents, contemplates guidance
upon this alien terrestrial plane, giggling
in the midst of our plight, catching God's breath.

*Such an insistent infant, pleasant servant of hope
to the distressed . . . She, bathed in innocence, knows nothing
of the world's faring. Still, she, at her current transient status,
reaches to care, shine the Will of her unseen source—
first Lover, whom she still kisses—to us.*

My daughter, by her mother's leave, will brush away
pieces of hate while painting on canvases scenes
of rhymes of compassion, and instruct the self-destructive
with a talent for predicting Sunday's outcomes
due to Friday's follies.

*A wise aberration in a consistently dark nation with
conflicting states stitched, dissolving; the body unhealed,
she'll bear the nobility of her Father's surname, exalting.
She'll be a tranquil symbol—green amid blue—lifting
a lamp for the lost on sad and dead seas, leading
a transition through*
flash floods, untamable currents, declawing crawlers,
corralling wild horses, shepherding them into their proper stables.

*It's weird we were struck with this same revelation seven
days ago: Two Infinite Trinities—God, man, and woman plus
woman, man, and child—equals a golden ring.*

We've sensed the presence of an embodiment of wisdom
holding a connection for Creation's completion.
Until she can claim her own name,
let's call her "Salam."

REHEARSAL
(Hanid's Secret Teaching)

Urn this to earn: Time to free, cash Family chips,
rescue those who'll sip, swallow anything laid on their lips.
David's last name translates from a sacred language into "Death."
What girl should share his breath?

Worms, study well. This is the final lesson preceding the Test.
Save the eloquence for bonus essays; for oral exams, brevity is best.
Know the theory, practice of hypothetical, hypocritical ethics.
Tick on pedantic antics.

Pursue and subdue
souls trained black, eyes strained blue.
This grimy season, robbery counts as no crime.
Our enclaved gathering
may've some not ready to sing.
Ventilate; I'll motivate, relate with rhyme:

Fellow dissidents, it's time to throw temples down.
A time to capture and bind those who mislead us around,
sacrifice lives on altars with a promise of life,
with one unsanitary knife.

Shepherds guide sheep to a slaughter of the sick,
making threats backed by gestures, waving wands and loaded sticks.
Heat swarms despite the fans (disseminating incense)—
congested pipes, watery eyes, lost conscience.

Esoteric wisdom in chains.
Powdered gloves miss-saging brains.
Drops of sweat outweigh tears.
Head coverings and robes,
ears pierced on the lobes—
signs of slaves, faithful for seven years.

A time to arouse, a time to liberate kin.
A time to blind pupils, look away from gods looking like men.

Pious garb and flowery dress worn to impress houseguests;
in their eyes, the wearer's blessed.

Choirs of angels sing their praises out loud,
clap, whistle, and dance, throwing shouts out in the crowd.
Intents to save a soul with a performance onstage;
success only in making once-sound sleepers enraged.

Shallow pool immersions,
enticing diversions
from steps, ladders, elevators, and stairs.
Hierarchies fall here
among all, drowned in fears
of death, when Truth meets their stares.

A time to arise, a time to cross burning sands.
A time to put property proper, know again our own lands.
Theocracies dictate where and how we should bleed,
forbidding us to read.

Rituals of rewards, offering tithes to the hilt,
sins of Sabbath eve cleansed, silver coins pay for guilt.
Organizations organized to feed the ass-masses lies;
drummed dumb; docile; no upstarts; no tries.

Unholy book burnings,
text twisting, limit learning
of facts from history past.
Indoctrinate children,
conceive idols and build them.
"Pay glory to our creations we cast!"

A time to understand, a time to raise wisdom high.
A time to come to the Zenith of how to live, give some to die.
A New Order I see beyond these clouds, cells solar
. . . . . Justice will call bluffs, snuff David's star.

THE SCRAMBLE

After dinner:
Mint for the halitosis,
fowl soul surviving past the most recent repast
featuring a roasted lamb, lame in life.
A coy steer; searing, staring away the coypu to the bay.
Baying at the moon, coyote, promotion to eagle over an ocean.

Skinny dipped in his native wild to propagate and initiate
a recruiting drive for the Family. Plane away. David's plain play:
to bull him into peril (the Poet needs fresh inspiration)
while our marriage is ruin-insured in a ten-minute town chapel
harem-ceremony.

Seems unseemly, but for the sake of Salam . . .
Less stress, hassle, irritation—rub the balm around the bruises
about my thighs.

Search and seize her, place the tot near the cots to witness
the repulsive scene with these teens (as the God-creature lurches
into a seizure in our room on Xyn's second floor) so she may insure
convulsions don't exceed the Spirit's bleeding-needs.

During the hustle-tussle, my thoughts are hassled
with the illusory ills of Hanid: on the poets' peak, shot down
to the valley of verses. As sex hastens, fastens, makes elusive thoughts
to exist, Hanid, fleshed, flustered, breaks in then, swinging fists.
Stripped to just shorts, his enmity unhemmed him.

Screaming "Fraud!", spilling spittle and cardinal-liquids,
Hanid eagerly testifies to his iconoclastic past, punching, scrunching,
lifting a bewildered deity, repeatedly, to the air.

He'd skipped the flight, doubled back to lock horns, lending himself
as an Enemy of Harmony, his main interest to keep quick-launching
David and landing him, unchecked,
on his neck.

Egalitarian pose: God and man, chattery chattels, scuffle, flip, switch
twisted. While the other girls, as they cringe, holler on the fringe,
I hold Salam, both of us unescaped, agape at the rodeo that cramped
an infinite trinity into a dueling duo. The ruckus breaks wood, bends
metal, smashes a lamp . . . two even on David's head.
On this fallen one, supported only by a bedpost,
the Poet pulls his pistol.

One of those who doesn't work well under order,
only within, or on, anarchy—
a girl of thirteen—kicks it from his hand.

In the Poet's baffle, David charges, tackles,
shackles with the cuffs the sadist planned for one of us.

Condemning him to starve in the Xyn prison,
David curse-reverses Hanid's image, rearranges his letters.

No pity; I'm no companion
to compassion for the hypocrite.
What was the greedy meaning of this speckled debacle?
We had both discussed, agreed to let David think Salam his baby
for reasons of non-aggravation, mutual "safety."

> *So he waffles . . .*
> *Can I digest this disgust?*
> *Eupepsia churned . . .*
> *My last lunch, lost.*

AGE, VENT; ADVANTAGE

Who will visit my shop, sit and swap,
before the pirates' bottling battleship sails,
heists, sells my share to atheist artists of fortune?
Maybe one of cupidity will come to raid, open this vault,
seeking to get gold-paid. Knocked out cold. Trade:
he can be me; I, him.

Before locked down, confused and abused by my sick muse,
she deemed to tell-kill me: *"You'd better repent, apologize to the Father*
for double-crossing his heart; come back to the Family."
Redemption, ruddy.

She—possessive of me, submissive to him.
I'm viciously banished, expected to deliciously vanish
as the vermin of minutes take pounds from my flesh,
puts them in my ears. From first to last, best to worst.
Four purposes crossed:
Lessen the worth of religious worship to entertain.
I pray only to, in their eyes, exit sane, less.

At this unctuous junction, I can but dye, pen an opus of protest,
on hope it's extant after later. Allegorical testimony, shrouded in a tale
of esoteric erotica: DEATH & LOVE—an epos of Passion.
Let me lose my voice in the roses my muse chooses. May the unholy see
an amazed and crazed artist persistently consisting of content,
simultaneously within: genius (fully) and madness (totally).

Junk or unction, may my shibboleths allow me to elope
into the readers', reciters' hearts, exhilarating auxiliary bodies . . .

Outside the iron door . . . .

I hear loud breathing . . . . .

BURNING THE OIL

Research in the archives of lives reviled and defiled
may reveal the real rival who truly deserves to be severely
severed and disposed
into the sewage of the servile.

Regathered my composure after a tossing, turning night
spotlighting a nasty, unchoreographed dance to the violent
scratching and mewing of violins. Refusing to register, a paralysis
of dismay from the display rendered me helpless during this crisis
of regents. But later, calm and kissing analysis,
the ramifications for the goat, unescaped,
crammed into my head, goaded, thrust me
into the Information Age.

Forced by my conscience to burn the post-midnight oil
on the counter of the spy. My sources: old articles
from the Waycross public library
collaborating with Xyn's private files.

A Sibling has written, in the Old Order, Solomon, the unsullied culprit,
Hanid's unaccomplished accomplice, was known as "the Recorder,"
David's solicitor of the disaffected from bookstores. In those days,
David's sermons used ostentatious musical theatre epics as a backdrop
to dramatize the narrative of the world's near-future demise
initiated by a greedy, red government.

Played too close to home, concern, wonderment, and other ornaments
decorated the minds of the Family when David planted a tree symbolizing
a New Order. According to the Recorder, the Family's new life asked men
to sacrifice their wives to David's loins.

Solomon obeyed, gave his first wife over to the new way,
but duplicitously drowned himself in spirits in a Waycross pub
—a hangout where he met his second wife-to-be, ask-masked
as a former mayor's daughter.

With Solomon under the influence, she had no trouble
eliciting the whole sorry tale.

Repulsed by his familial affiliation, she dragged him away from Waycross
and had him deprogrammed. But, the later marriage was a sham:
she, a con-woman who marries and, before divorcing,
sues for spousal abuse,
or so it was reported in the local paper
sporting objective news.

Solomon went on to found a rival sect to David's Family.
The world-worshipping followers in his small theatre troupe recruit
whom they can in tiny towns. Caring nothing big for his children
fathered through seven plus three uncommon law wives, Solomon instead
rewards his regard upon the gullible cynics and old crickety critics
who, ignoring the lack of true value in Solomon's half-hearted partial
art and fueled by the energy of his heresy, cry for the authorities
to prematurely gather and redistribute
the Loves hanging on David's living tree
. . . or so the Children have imparted to me.

EXTRACT FROM THE NATION'S CAPITAL'S NEWSPAPER

". . . experts exert the Xynite leader believes he's an earthbound god
above all secular laws. 'He distrusts the State that trusts in the true God,'
said a local ecclesiastic who's advising the Bureau on cult mentality.
'He thinks he's the one who's been sent to purify the planet. Then,
a grand cosmic jury will deem him fit to rejoin the universal Entity.'

"Hardly harmless eccentrics, there're reports of incest—
brothers and sisters copulating with each other and the 'father,'
a bisexual child molester. All claiming a divine driver's license
to find, found a '13ᵗʰ Tribe of Xynites to go forth and subdue.'
On an Isis basis:
                    Women are subjected, pressed into the sole-roles of procreators.
Both they and their pre-teen babies are forced into the labors
of cooking, sewing, and cleaning.

"Abused, deprived of public school classes and radio, television broadcasts.
'Kidnapping and braincleaning are the most minor of their crimes,'
said an insider known only as 'the Sheriff.'
                                'They've been modifying their compound
into a fortress, steady readying for protracted war against the State.'
Gun-toting fanatics, stockpiling machine guns, automatic weapons.

"'Behind an invisible shield of dignity, the insider's steadfast integrity
allowed him to dig past, deep into their trust while remaining loyal to us,'
said a Bureau spokesperson. 'We've learned
                        they've a methamphetamine lab,
a greenhouse for producing, growing drugs to sell.
Collaborating with Mexico, three hundred miles from their base,
                        they've established a drug-baby trade.
The unsaleable babies, growing to children, are ritually sacrificed
—they've some prophecy about 'blood in the desert.'"

"Dead years of red tears: Why hasn't a squad moved to impound
these heinous murderers? 'Couldn't construct a case. We had spurious
rumors but no proof until we placed our own puck, spurred by the local
yokels picketing in Waycross, hanging SOS signs on their fences
and pickup trucks.

"'The cult was passed over by the census, though everyone knows they exist.
Wading through supranatural fear, we had to find a temporal judge to rile,
scratch with the rusty nails of women and children kept as hostages in fetid,
squalid pools and pens. Allaying his temper—us, promising tetanus shots—
the judge endorsed a form saying they've squandered their squatter's rights
by dodging the payment of taxes on firearms, unregistered.

"'We're mobilizing a surprise, so keep your senses clear, smart.
We're preparing our props; soon it'll be showtime!'"

CRADLESONG
(Shariah's Private Prayer)

Secreting milky secrets to you, dear daughter,
                                    to hush your doubtful pouting.
My insatiable pudgy fudge . . . Why do you continue on
with these ominous yawns foreboding odious calamities?

                    Calm yourself, callow.
Call low; stall your calls out as I confess in an acappella fashion:

Hear:
You are not the first past zero but first past twelfth child
sired by David.
Here, in my presence, reared.

                    I've lied by the Truth so often
to soften the feelings
of my Hanid.

Half-breeds, you and I: There's optimistic intelligence and experience
crossed with dour mysticism. I hope your crossed eyes never cause the foolish
to look upon you with distrust or disinterest. Those who fear a free society
won't want their sight
to smile on you.

There, my dear . . . Release that gas. It will pass, this anxiety, like a ghost
through the frightened, aghast gates. Here . . . Let me wipe that crust
from your chin. I see you're anxious to push the extra milk
out your nostrils again.

Grief or grace, never forget your true place: to mitigate, apply balm
to those scalded. Scold those insipid ones who heated the cold water
and dipped, sipped, thinking it would be conducive
to humanity's well-being.

Keep your powerfully tender syllables in a vocal cab, ready to travel;
caress the wailing, finesse, bail the ailing from their anti-human prisons.
Be genuine and gentle under your four-wheel-driven awning as you heal,
telling the passengers their next stop may be the spirit realm or hell,

the animal's plant world
or a newborn's mind and skin.

Begin again to sing of good fortune.
This baby oil will easy-please your skin
to the silent sights listening, observing,
and absorbing so they too may glisten.

Know as you grow and seek golden truths:
The most convincing evidence is personal experience.
You may prosper if your temper doesn't rise above your peers.

Silence . . .
> *Your fears, staid; in your stead, no one will plead for humankind*
save for some who believe in instant relief. Instead,
believe enough that you can accomplish more in your Way,
as within it you have already achieved—your timbre trimming
timber to construct this cradle.

One song I hope not to pass on:
The tapping of drums backed by a choir of twenty-four.
The thumping conundrums must have been your beating heart,
heard from the death of classmates,
ceased at your birth . . .
> *shush, shush.*

You may feel swollen now in your swaddling clothes . . .
Shhh . . .
> *I'll hum . . .*
Just swallow, close your eyes . . .
> *Imagine:*

One lamb jumps, escapes a gallows . . .

Two lambs . . .

HOLOCAUST

Hell, come home.

In the pale month of visible breath, the month of Death and Love:
I've entered into the post-trance, after the séance.

In the vault: Skin, flesh, experience withering away: becoming sentient
to the sixth or the seventh degree; and I, assuming the guise of José,
Brother, horticulturalist, and ex-friend. Beyond that, beyond—
going, goings on. Unseen in here; hearing, seeing their reality:

I, as a hosted ghost, have escaped the vault, my palliative prison
on the other side of the Center's cafeteria. Assumed dead, if not forgotten,
I amble through narrow halls, shouldering a head with a mindsight
of super-presence; the delirium in my skull (bone-walled sanitarium)
processes this experience:

Operation on white, red, and black Trojan horses:
Time has shown the seals being torn, shredded, and thrown up to rain down
as confetti. Parties of words read, ideas spread. Our religion is one
of water and light, which outsiders have mistaken for ferocious fire.
But, they say, who in their right mind could find our left-behind light, on
the edges, on the margins of a rationalizing society?

On Mound Xyn, houses of individuals were being processed
on the property, demolished in order that one communal building
might be constructed from their parts. Before my incarceration,
I took part in this, as did all male and a few female Family members.

Recycling process complete; but there're still bubbles of rubble about,
spied by some of my eye-thoughts that are floating above, surveying
the grounds. Scoping for trouble around, down, down the lane, a truck
is coming, running, speeding, driven by one of ours. A Brother
who works as a postal carrier in town, Billy seems harried, hurried,
worried as he haphazardly parks his vehicle and sprints out towards
the door with a newspaper in hand. A few of my eye-thoughts descend,
follow, as Billy, blustered, hustles inside.

Finding David with three others, all Brothers, Billy rushes with this:
"Listen! On my route, just now, some out-of-town newsman stopped me.
He asked for directions to the 'Devil's Anthill.'"

"What's that?" asks David.

"Here," Billy replies; "Look at this!"

He shows them a copy of the Capital Newspaper featuring an article
fussing about us and warning of an impending siege.

"As soon as I saw this, I hurried back here.
On the way, I passed a station wagon, filled with soldiers . . .
They were heading in this direction!"

David takes a deep breath, releases, and smiles. He turns
to one of his companions, shakes his hand, says, "Sheriff, you must do
with this dust what you must," and points him towards the front door.

The "Sheriff," embarrassed, but without harassment, makes it to, out,
and away.

"You just let him go?" a bewildered Billy blows. "He was an infiltrator,
a spy—one who no doubt spoon-fed these journalists for their shitty lies!"

"He's part of the Plan, the Will," David whispers with a chill. "Now,
go prepare the others."

And they run off, save for one Brother who stays with David
as they walk to peer out of a window.

I—not so slow, nor so low—can see and read with up-high eye-thoughts
a convoy a mile long speeding towards Mound Xyn. Sandwiched
in-between this dry, flowing stream are a couple of cattle trailers
being hauled by bulky trucks. The condiment vehicles (gassing and
steaming) carry at least eighty Agents geared for combat: video cameras,
guns and similar unfun weapons, nylon handcuffs, and flashy grenades.

Circling the communal structure—I'll resist using the analogy of vultures
—but my educated memory mumbles something about cowboys circling
the camp of redmen dissenters. The Agents, sporting blue-black uniforms

emblazoned with bold yellow signature call letters, jump from their wheeled
nooks, pour from the dry stream that ran and just defied further laws
by becoming an above-ground moat. Six snipers surround the community;
three armed, motorized dragonflies hover; and daft journalists with
agendas converge, hoping to draft epitaphs for the living devils
they developed then deviously exposed.

Inside the communal building, women and children run to the second
(and highest) floor—the level that weapons, women, children, and David
claim as their resting pad. Most go into the kids' rooms; others run
towards the base of the residential minaret at the back of the upper floor.

The cattle trailers park in front of the building;
among all those hustling, two agents stand
and rattle steely words.

David opens the westward entrance door and walks out
with his hands up, saying, "Wait! What's this? Let's talk!
There're women and children inside!"

One Agent bellows, "Police! Shut up! Get down!"
And another, "Ram it!"

Agents begin to advance.
David turns, re-enters, and slams the door.

With no disruption in time flow, or even motion slow, gunfire erupts,
fly-crashing, smashing through the windows and doors, and David
and a Brother, drop, hit. Mutual rat-at-tat-attack heard by patriots
and spiritualists around the flowery-colored world.

Agents run, taking cover behind a cream van and a white picket fence,
seeking the safety of its cinder block base from the bullets, hitting,
pelting, shot from the Mound Xyn shelter Center, targeting
the blue-black yellow-callers.

With several big bangs, it began; it begins in and around the inner galleries,
the prairies, over and under barriers, small and minor artillery
causing explosions of space, effecting collapses in space. Back and forth,
forward attacks—iron and steel horsemen and horsewomen saddle
little gadget-laden behemoths.

Outside, hulking warships rev, as inside, junior reverends worship
the God they love and trust by raining armor-piercing fire down upon
the Transnational Adversary. From the roof, and tower, first and second
story windows, Xyn's men and some women pray with grimaces
for God to ambush these menaces. By his wealth of power, stealthily
stalking with yellow silence among the sagebrush and Texas flowers,
this was the hour for the golden Deity to come to their aid.

But my free-roaming eye-thoughts see, know that the health of the Father
is not up to the task of engaging in this moral war. David is bleeding
badly; he was shot several times. One of the Brothers is screaming
into the telephone at a police department official, trying
to convince him to call off the raid. Negotiations of sorts—sports;
horseshoes tossed from post to post: "Call it off!
We've got women and children here!
They won't stop firing!"

"Who?"

"I don't know! Them! Out there! The Feds . . .
tell them to stop! We've got people shot!"

Too excited to get anything clear across or righted,
so a calmer Brother takes the phone and continues in a more sedated tone:
"We've got people hurt here. Send an ambulance . . .
and call off the damn raid!"

"How many men shot?"

"I don't know . . .
A few."

"What's 'a few'?"

"Generally speaking, more than two . . ."

"And specifically speaking?"

"I think three."

"Where?"

"Here!"

"There?"

"Dammit! Call it off!"

The mercenary agency continues to show no leniency—the one-
minute lulls in gunfiring is the set-up for the Agents to toss in grenades,
flashbangers that clash with human wholeness, mutilating bodies
by blowing off hands and feet.

The grenades produce terrific blinding lights, horrific rackets.
Among the terrors and horrors, shooting and shouting, I see
some pious children hiding under their beds, hum-mumbling prayers
with their anxious, frightened mothers.

Outside, Agents try to scale the building, using twenty-foot ladders
of aluminum, trying to get on top of Xyn, trying to get inside, trying to find
(from what I hear) our empty gunroom.

In one room, two Sisters, principals, debate the principles of peace:
One armed with a double-barreled shotgun, standing guard at the window,
the other, nursing her baby, cursing and crying as she crouches behind
pillows in the corner. The cornered animal, hording panicked insanity
like a criminal, maws on about the flaws in divine laws
that would allow such an assault on Shariah—herself, her concern
on wealth.

The hordes of foes amassed, the sinners and false beginners passed
—why o spell, God do tell, why the more faithful and innocent
suffer more?

Then, this ghost, from gassy thoughts and organs re-gathered (structured
and solidified, back as one), moved by the scene, I glide.

True, it's my wife;
regardless of what she did in my past life, I care for her,
and for my daughter even more.

Through the door, I walk to ask what I may offer.
One step in, a flashbanger mirrors my entrance, in through the window.

Dodging, then repositioning, the armed woman cocks, fires scattershot.
I run for, hit the floor, grab the grenade, and fling it into the hall.

"Thanks, José," the guard gasps without looking as she struggles to reload.
But Shariah sees through all, stops cursing and stands tall. Looking me
in the face, she furrows her brow.

"Hanid?
You escaped?
Why are you dressed up like a gardener?"

Before I can afford her a plausible response, the other woman
fires her shotgun, killing one Agent, and maybe another, nicking him,
knocking him for a great fall off his ladder. Someone returns fire,
one of the six snipers, missing the killer, but hitting Shariah in her temple.

Blood spatters on my face,
some drips on Salam,
and the succeeding sequence begins to proceed with a carelessly muted,
stuttering eloquence:

I think to reach for the collapsing body,
but my muscles aren't functional.
An idiopathic spirit seizes my extremities and coils within,
traveling up my limbs—
coiling, coiling, slithering, and spoiling
my blood, making me twitch and fitch, move erratically,
here and there—idiosyncrasies. Bending, cringing
(thanks to a thousand internal twinges),
forearms and calves no longer recognizing
elbows and knees as hinges.
The coiling continues around my trunk,
squeezing, holding,
emboldening—spine, ribcage,
re-barked, reinforced; on its course
the spirit has me, has it:
the fruit my skull protected.
And I know, I feel, in all
seven branches to my temples,
the Quickening: blood iron, skin steel,
liquid blackness, blocky,

shocking, clock-rocking: twenty-two dualities
experienced in fractional seconds. In two hells;
dueling tales—bifurcated spirit-force
in one fleshy tool. Hell: low.
Hello. Halo
revolving about my swelling pate:
a rainbowed reptile eating its own tail.
Quickening; sickening—split,
quartered . . .
restoration to Order.

While this took place, the Sister with the shotgun
had dropped it and scooped up Salam in her arms.
Cuddling, coddling, comforting, she had run
from the room to find her other children
—hopefully safe—and make an addition.
Another tot to care for. A lot to watch over.

I walk to the window in time to see a shot Agent fall from the roof.
The remaining Agents of the assault team up there fire down
methodically through the ceiling. What of their intelligence?
They can only know they're aiming for rooms of tots and cots,
women and linen. What about the men? Most are down below,
withstanding other blows: Wrists, biceps, and thighs needlessly needled;
stomachs pumped with lead; blunt objects uncorrecting heads.
The three motorized dragonflies swoop and swipe by,
alternating passes, switching chances to fire down into the room
over our chapel and our residential tower. Family members retaliate,
striking down two of the flies (forcing them to seek rest and recuperation
in a nearby field), but only wounding another, leaving it with enough
strength to bullet our water tank, draining it with riddles,
and to mow down our furry guards, pets,
and friends for the children.

David cautiously walks on the overhead way above the chapel.
I feel compelled to say something,
but as I take my hand and make a stand,
pots drop,
prods stop,
and David is shot
either by the men up above,

or the remaining hovering,
buzzing fly.

He screams, scrunches, hunches,
grabs his right hand and collapses
as I again am seized
with a stiffening internal winter breeze:

Seduced into trying to cry, an edible bulb of an idea,
biting and licking layer and layer and layer and layer;
devouring levels of the vegetable, each one inducing
multiple more tears to wash, a seawatery universal solution.

Thirty-three trinities enfold, unfold, and fold me into myself,
helping harmony between spirit and matter, force and form, reform.
Two rainbowed rings now silently sing
as they spin,
alternating the sides on which they tilt.

Not too soon after, after two hours, the shots die out
—a ceasefire finally has been talked into existence, ordered,
in order that all sides may take collections.

Of the Agents, four are dead;
they're carried from our premises (far from where we shed fire)
to a hospitable watershed. For lack of ambulances, they are slung,
draped, balanced on the hoods of trucks.

All injured among the Family refuse to be carried or ferried away
for outside medical aid.

Ailing—thirty-two on both sides are wounded with gashes and slashes
by windows' glass shattered by flying bullets; skin punctures and fractured
bone junctures by those same leaden buzzers. Head and shoulders and,
above the rest of the appendages, the buttocks and legs bleed for bandages.

Of ours, six were slaughtered, three and three casualties counted: in our
water tower, a Brother armed only with a rust chipper; another armed
with a plastic fork intending to attack and torture French toast
in the private chamber of his room; the Brother who accompanied David
to the door; an unknown Brother in David's sleeping room

on the fourth floor of the tower; a Sister running through the hall, calling
for her children; and Shariah—
Won now:

My muse is simply me divided by us.

David's wounds are not fatal, but severe—diced in the wrist,
the nerve to his thumb was severed, and a bit of his hipbone
was also sliced. Jittering, dittering, moving in and out of consciousness
and pain, he looks at us through blood-stained, steamed glasses and cracks
a quick joke, adamantly refuses aspirin, and offers a serious line
of encouragement to the fretting, mournful Brothers and Sisters
surrounding him.

A Sister who works as a nurse in Waycross checks and confirms
his blood pressure is uncomfortably low. It's like this for an hour,
out and in, as we pace, watching him turn paleface, and his eyes shake
and roll back further into his head. Suddenly, at sixty (give or take
three) minutes, he shouts for his guitar, waits, and once it's given,
he spins off a new song
no one's heard before.

All the while, a rotation of four Brothers stays on the phone to maintain
the ceasefire, negotiate, and gather information. No one notices or makes
any remarks regarding my escape from the vault. No one addresses
or recognizes me as anyone other than José
—a thin disguise masking a rich combination.

In the afternoon, our dead count goes up to seven as we hear
of a Brother who was hit earlier off the premises. He was shopping
in Waycross when the raid began. On his way back, he hit a roadblock
and was forced to try to enter the Center from an obscure trail.
He was observed, caught,
and shot in the back.

The Next Day:
The Investigators join the Agents.
On the night before, the mad media, who came with the Agents,
were pushed back to a three-mile radius around Mound Xyn.
The Agents and Investigators stare at us from but yards away.
David sings to us of his prophecy:

"The Adversary surrounds the camp; the Saints will die.
There will be blood and fire, an explosion at the end."

As some Brothers venture outside to collect water, they notice
the Investigators securing their positions with gun posts and moving
fighting vehicles. The showdown, the standoff, the show-offs:
Surrounded by the four (times many men and women more)
horsepersons absent bullhorns
heralding the coming of the EndWar.

Through their correspondence, our despondent negotiators
have learned the real bottom reason behind this turn;
when asked and pestered by us, they respond:
"Something about us possessing unregistered firearms
that they want to inspect, stuff we're supposed to pay taxes on.
They say they're holding a warrant. They say they're also holding
the key to our lives. The ransom they want is David. That's it.
They want to arrest him."

Then why the need for distorted news articles
and this show of preposterous proportions?
And why didn't they arrest him, peacefully,
during his daily jaunt to town or his occasional
but unrare sunrise constitutionals? David answers me:
"They chose not to do so in order that the prophesied
sacrifice might take place."

In the evening, David calls us all around and tells us he has passed
a message that he will surrender in the morning. He also makes it clear
that each of the rest of us should feel free to make the choice to leave
in groups or individually at any time before David's departure or after;
we don't have to act in exact concordance with him.
Most say they will elect to stay
until God clearly expresses otherwise.

The Next Day:
As was negotiated, David broadcasts a sermon over the radio airwaves
on the subject of "Higher Justice: Love & Forgiveness."
After the hour-long diatribe, he and we begin to make preparations
to surrender. He disappears into his room while we pack necessities
and ready the children. Twenty minutes later, he emerges with this blow:

"God says 'no.'
We must wait."

So negotiations on the telephone are relit and burned, raging
on and on, profanities and blasphemies exchanged quite freely.
David keeps in play his offer that anyone in the Family may leave
the Center at any time, except for those vined to him by both blood
and wine. In spite of agitation for the hazy future and frustration
at the all-too-vivid present,
most stay in the lines.

Pass it; hooked tense;
look back and make sense:
Over the next several days came a demonstration of demolition.

Even though they spread the word that David and his acolytes
were holding men, women, and children as hostages against their will,
twenty-two did leave the Center to tell them contrary. Instead of being
heard, these people were handcuffed, gagged, and imprisoned
—except for the children,
who were separated
from their parents' supervision.

Despite promises to send the care-packaged kids to their relatives,
they were herded to governmental daycare facilities
where they were coerced to eat unclean foods, consume acidic
and toxic beverages, and be programmed by mind-numbing
television broadcasts. When the children protested, citing their religion,
the government goons sneered and scared the tykes by massaging
threats of beheadings
into their psyches.

Meanwhile, closer to home, the Agents and Investigators began to close
their circle around the Mound Xyn Center by several meters each day
—smashing outbuildings and ramming our motor vehicles. Their tanks
trashed Billy's mobile home, crushed kids' go-carts, flattened trikes
and bikes, crashed into our fishing boat, and went digging and sprigging
in the cemetery on our privately owned land.

Snatching and enslaving our children, imprisoning our Family members,
laying waste to our property—this three layered angel's food cake

was frosted with obscene gestures (finger flippings, pale cheek moonings,
and abrasive expletives) directed at any man, woman, or child who made
the mindless mistake
of peeking out of the window.

The slaying of days, the peaks and squeaks of weeks, sun and moon
on and on: Threats and promises continued to be batted back and forth
over the phone lines—some were fulfilled,
some chilled (to be reheated later),
and some killed.

Radio reports told us the world knew of our plight,
but public support of spiritual freedom and religious minorities
was out of fashion for the current cycle of nights. It seemed all reporters
reported stories of folks being displeased with the Freeman's Disease.
Commentators teased with delight that some mothers
were starting to discipline their babes with this fright:
"I'll send you down to Mound Xyn if you don't behave!"
And dazzled David, in his more manic raves, razzled the frazzled Family
by threatening to send the problem adults out of the Center
into the arms of Babylon
if they didn't act right.

In spite of the increasingly caustic stylings of this cautious mystic,
my inimical feelings towards him have rapidly decreased. Earth to heaven
starland translation: He has been holding fast as a buffer, suffering
for Xyn's Family—he might even say he was doing this for "humanity."
Blood pressure maintaining its abysmal level, consciousness and stability
uncontrollable: one hand on life, the other on death—the bleeding soft line
or vessel of muscle and skin that connected one world with another,
he prays of life, he sings of eternity, he converses with some unknowns
to deliver us, with or without him, to a peaceful place of sanity.

The Agents, Investigators, and other Instigators want David dead,
and quickly done; sickly David wants us to live, alone with Love, forever.

This Knowledge came under my possession in a past instant,
but Understanding it has been a slow progression. As a result
of the intense feeling that Wisdom feeds, I have taken it upon myself
to maintain a constant position of defense for this man, standing by
the window nearest him, armed, keeping a hawk-eye for snipers,

a nose for vapors, and an eye for traitorous backbiting capers, although
there's little I can do to stave the bloody urine and splitting migraines
of which he complains. The spasms and tremors continue to unzip
and rip open the wounds on his skin, and he inevitably trips and slips
in and out of coherency and consciousness.

Time passes wind and gasses as, due to bargaining and the exercise
of free minds, eighteen other Family members departed from the Center.
Unbalanced, deceived, we realized the Adversary was sending in
little in exchange, nothing we really needed. Milk and medical kits
were items we got that were among the most wanted. But our attitudes
became expressed by rude rantings as we discovered the Adversary
was planting on these items bugs that relayed our sentences and moving
mug shots back to their command center. Of course, though, knowing
Xyn was infested months before, I couldn't move myself to get as peeved
as most of the rest.

For food, we survived on meals of popcorn, nuts, water,
applesauce, raisins, rolls, and our collection of chickens
that we had kept penned in the back, graciously spared
by the sons of bitches who murdered our dogs.

Used to keeping lights off at night for fear of being shot, it was
an unpleasant but not an impossible adjustment when the enemy
disconnected our heat and electricity, forcing us to huddle, cuddle,
and keep warm over kerosene lanterns, propane heaters, and two
generators that drank plenty of gasoline.

Our luck, it dwindled,
as did the water supply outside.

For relief, we could only use buckets and pails,
which we dumped in the underground passageways under the Center.
Each journey down there, the journeymen would search for something
to bolster the bales of hay we had stacked against the inside walls
of our building to protect us from outside gunfire.

When land was scanned and a new cemetery planned on which
we could agree (and enough free courage was mustered by some stalwart
souls to go out under the cover of night to do the damned deed) fresh graves
were dug for the six dead. Improper burial, but it was still our property.

Not only this, but all the nights were freezing. Texas winds are nice-icy,
but the Adversary tried to warm us with their cheer. Making up
for the discontinued electricity, they began to shine stadium lights
on the building, overwhelming the paucity of our lanterns and candles.

They also began a curious serenade of furious sounds: Helicopters
hovering, locomotives governing, dentists' drills preparing for fillings,
shrill roosters crowing, cows mooing, bluesy bag pipes blowing, busy
telephones signaling, tapes of week-old negotiations playing the talks,
squawking birds, clocks ticking, and the squeals of quick bunnies
being passionlessly slaughtered
several weeks before their time.

A Brother who had seen wars before this, worse than this
(and, yes, it's a war, a segment of one greater, universal)
explained that this is the crowning tactic used in some "Psyche-Wars"
—to drive the beleaguered into a sad craziness
the propagandists and perpetrators have long insisted
they had already inescapably delved deep into.
It's to make fulfilling truth of their earlier empty lies.

After asking them to curtail the wails, to no avail,
we plotted our counterattack. When they began the second round
the following week, subjecting us to amplified prayer calls, chants, carols,
and classic "Top 40 hit songs," we put batteries in our cassette players,
hooked them up to our concert speakers, and turned and tuned them
to give the Adversary a demonstration, at full blast,
of what the Xyn's performing reformers once had planned to unleash
upon the world: recordings of our new wave gospel music
and singing designed to convert and recruit potential Family members
before the final Apocalypse.

This sufficiently countered the bombardment
from the Adversary's speakers,
until the juice from our batteries ran out.

But we didn't.
And out of frustration,
and in retaliation,
they snipped our telephone lines, thereby calling an end to the negotiations
and our communication with the world outside of the Center. Before this,

a total of forty Family members—sinking to believing the thieves
and thinking they would better understand the bandits—had left
the Mound and gone down to be arrested. At the cutting of the cords,
we settled into self-suspension and voluntary detention.

No more of us would leave.

The Adversary began to send us messages in a different manner.
Shortly before they gave up on their sound and music tactics, they
hoisted high two of their barn-side banners to intimidate us: Old Glory
and a white flag with two diagonally crossing red stripes.

Then as a grand finale for their songshow,
at the highest volume they could achieve,
they played a profanity-laden version of the Doodle song, adding
another accursed verse to the jingled song that's already overweight
with 299.

David, in a lurid moment, whispered to those of us who attended
to him that we were in the fifth of the seven scriptural seals—
our seven Brothers and Sisters who had died
were at rest during the current season; David informed us that he met
and conversed with them during his unconscious modes.
But when this season ends, the whole Family will be reunited in white
and God will take vengeance upon the Adversary.

"This trying Tribulation will last, in total, a week
for every one hundred Lawless Officers that currently encircle our home."

Peering out the window, I slowly realized I couldn't count that high
while standing up. It may've been the multitude outside
or the lack of food inside that dizzied me, forcing me to sit down,
perhaps preparing me for another, but minor, withering experience.

Others around me experienced dithering issues of their own.
David, when conscious, noticed this and prayed for our deliverance.
He knew what had to pass, but he begged God for another route,
a way out.

He declared he'd gladly drink,
but only if promised the rest of us would be drenched in sunshine

for a time longer on this wretched planet. Then one night,
I heard him issue an ultimatum to God: "You have seven days,
or I quit."

Seven days from David's demand on the Deity, he sent out a mother
and her son to tell the Adversary that he will come out, peacefully,
only under two conditions: if he is allowed to finish his final pop opera,
STAR STORY, and if he is assured a publisher who will make the work
readily available, for free,
to the public.

The work, David confided to us, is an analysis,
a translation of the seven seals as foretold in the scriptures,
as revealed to him. When meditated upon by humankind,
it will operate to reveal all necessary truths to them.
Fame through famine, starvation. The retardation of art
for the spirit's salvation, superstar-status.

As the mother and child deliverers were arrested
as soon as they approached the enemy's perimeter,
we had no idea whether they accepted David's proposal or not,
or even whether they got the message.

So, a few times after that, David attempted to send other scouts
out to get the nuts and bolts of if they agreed
or sat steady on and within their iron and steel steeds. Apparently,
they were no longer greedy for Family feed; everyone we sent outside
was driven back into the Center by flashbangers.
Shooting ducks in a pond after tossing them bread crumbs.
No exit.

Others and I were perplexed by this;
and in my dreams, I dreamed of attacking blackness.

Present time (three-dimensional mind) rebinding me:
Black Monday opens with a sky streaked with crimson and azure.
I gaze beyond the paned glass at the Gathering—boatman, ferry on . . .

The cocky birds, early words—spits of crows on carrion: "The siege,
page over. We will be entering the building. Come on out, your hands up.
This is not an assault."

114

Bullhorns amplified, singsong singing, the undertoned dirge
intending to lull the dull as the tanks surge. Gunshine awaken,
most in the Family are stirred, shaken with the walls as the little behemoths
with thirty-foot booms attempt to knock-knock-enter the building.
Bullhorns sticking to it. Longsong still singing: "The siege, page over.
We will be entering the building. Come on out, your hands up.
This is not an assault."

This rings with the screams of the tanks backing on their tracks, then
forwarding, re-tracking to rock-rock the sheety walls of the Center,
penetrate our party, with their booms snorting and then zorting
some kind of white powder that sinks to the floor of our place.

David, with a rage that counters paralysis and pain, orders fires to be lit
strategically to destroy, counterthank the tanks. Mighty frightened men
run around like blind mice, looking to find the fathers feared by ice.

Before withdrawing, the three or four tanks batter, ram once more, again
pump-dumping in that powder which sinks, carpets our floor. David pumps
his lungs, limping about, shouting for the Fire Plan to be aborted
—but I doubt all his men are hearing him, seeing as how they ran far away
throughout the far reaches of the complex when he initialed
the primary order.

I leave my post and go quick-trip-skipping down the steps, being drawn
partially by reddish screams whipping a raspy-flavored cream from
the halls and unlocked rooms of my Team. Some children and women cry
that their skin is burning; on examination, I see blisters
—soon someone's running through, yelling a message to pass:
"The white stuff's tear gas! Don't touch it . . . Get the gas masks!"

Prevented by a fit of coughs, but I want to ask "Where?" Chest tightening,
I have to take a chair. Breaths get shorter, as clouds rise higher in the air.
Tear ducts reign; frontal lobe strained in pain. Sight not right, so I rely on
my eighth sense of success. It picks me up, carries me to the closest source
of human mass misery. On my way, Brother André tags me with a gas mask
—before I can hack up a "Thank You," he's off, helping the other helpless,
while the less afflicted pass, brush by me to hand out, secure other filters.

It's soon found, with uncrusted frustration,
the gas masks are too big for the little children's heads. Instead,

as a substitute, the mothers and women
place wet towels and soaked rags on their faces.

Thunderous poundings begin again, verbing, continuing to reverberate
throughout the building; ramming, rumbling of engines are all around.
I hear the squealing of the tank tracks, revealing the dirt; I still hear
the megaphone singsonging, backing up the lead screamers in here:
"We hereby usurp your authority, Dave. Consider yourself relieved
of godship. Submit to proper authorities!"

Stumbling along as the rumbles go on, I see tanks yanking hunks
and chunks from the walls of sheetrock of our dormitory block;
another tank, joining in the fun, pun-punches with its boom a hole
in the middle of the row of our sleeping rooms. Finally, I hear
some of the Brothers or Sisters opening fire out of fear.

Enticing responses, shells (filled with powdery gas) rocket
through the windows, shattering whatever is still pane-full of glass. Clear
tears on white pillows: the clouds of powdery gas billow throughout,
baking our skin, and caking and frosting the ceilings, floors, and walls.

Some rockets, before docking, explode on first impact. These acts
push some into an all-out frenzy. Down whatever halls, some women run
for shelter in the concrete cooler placed at the base of the tower of residents.
Some and their children remain under raggedy pretenses, under blankets,
huddling in the cold storage room in the middle
of our humble communal structure.

Wounded and bleeding, the Center, on itself, starts feeding. With shards
flying and laying, corridors of potential escape blocked and naysaying—
the walls all around begin to collapse. Sheetrock and timber—the debris,
in some areas, higher than the knees. But despite cries of *"God, please!"*
the scary knocking of the hairy predators continues.

I make my way to the chapel, now and still under direct attack.
Others have sought shelter here, and I stare, wondering what I should do
to help them out. A tank batters three times, belligerently, on the east wall.
After all move to the west side, it hesitates, then backs off. The crowd of us
reconvenes in the middle, sitting on the few pews that are still hospitable.
Some begin quoting verse and scripture, reassuring self or lecturing others,
while a few loners listen to the snowy waves over a transistor radio.

I hang with the latter group, until the crackling and popping
hacks on my last nerve and stops me—and I go from the chapel,
feeling more than solitary. Then something from above
hits the ceiling, quake-shaking all walls
and grounding the foundation.

Three hours since the attack began. Free-roaming eye-thought-spirits
homing, networking, spell-telling me that over four hundred rockets
have been shot into the Center; the heater has been crushed, spilled
lanterns unhushed propane and kerosene vapors; some last-minute
flashbangers are creating tiny, small fireballs. Colorlessly coated:
the remaining walls, floors, ceilings . . . a feeling, picked up, kicking up—
a wind, whipping at thirty miles an hour, breezing,
easing through a Center's wounds.

Then all, before the call, I'm told of three big exploding fireballs
simultaneously inspired in three separate places by the souls shaping
three different faces: In one, while poking holes in our walls, one
of the Adversary's attackers turned over a propane tank; in another,
some Brothers recalled David's earlier holler, and they sought
to fend off an attacker with fire; in the other, the third, the fireball's creation
is a mystery shrouded by part of me,
and forever will be
until a higher power presents my conscious self
with the skeleton key.

Spending with the wind, in all of eleven minutes,
the three disparate fireballs run through the building and converge.
An anonymous yell of *"Fire!"* also swells and spreads,
and everyone who's able begins to search for an escape route.

On my way, on my knees (but not thinking to pray), I crawl
up the stairs that will take me to the catwalk over the chapel
—the same walkway where David was shot.

Dodging stark falling shards and darkening debris (sky falling),
I crawl all the way across the walk to the other end, to a veiled opening,
possible draped escape. I come up on one knee and poke my top through,
only to have my cheeks torched, ears borched by the red, yellow, or orange
spherical lover of Phosphor.

Deaf now, I fall back, retracing my previous paced prints, glancing
down to catch the pantomime (no sound) of the folks in the chapel,
itself now on fire. They're in each other's arms, massed at the edge
of the platform for performance. Fireballs race and retrace
across the ceiling.

I jump down to meet my Family, descending into increasing heat, forcing
me to age—I've no choice now but to remove this gardener's garb,
a disguise for a grander stage. The artist's technique of dress-up, make-up,
and make-believe were taught to me by Sol's friends; but retracing acts,
who's the enemy to deceive? A thought in my head: They want us dead.
But define "they," refine "us."

Two Brothers then brush past me:
Hal and Gus. They run out of a challenging door, waving their arms
to catch a cab, hail a bus. They are greeted by those waiting behemoths
which, when seeing them, pick up nothing but speed, running down
the runners; gripping and grabbing the flab and whatever guts
under the abs, severing the right side of Gus's torso; and more mercifully,
not quite sharing the care for his pal, just shearing the leg of Hal, leaving
him to gasp, holler, pus out, and live for a while
(For a prayer? Making peace with the Taker?)
before backing over to sedate his misery.

Baking, I make my way to the concreted cold storage room,
hoping to find some safe and sheltered from harm.

Beyond alarm; dust-stormed farm: I find
five-squared dead tots and four-squared dead mothers, their bodies
deep in sleeping bags, intended, I'm assuming, for protection
from the snowy gas. But more than a couple, it's plain, have died
due to falling chunks from the ceiling after it was bombed. Alone
and alive among the mangled, slaughtered by starry-eyed animals,
is one child, one girl—amid a dead sea, a wild pearl. My daughter:
Salam.

I run, scoop the charmed darling in my arms, hugging, and she tugs
at my sleeves, gurgling what sounds like *"need."*

I step highly over bodies, clutching her, the retrieved treasure;
and moving out of the failed fort, fallen-out shelter, I just run straight,

with an awkward, hoppy, wobbling, hobbling, quicky gait;
my hearing is nearly beyond repair, and my sight is eager to get there.
So impaired, I bulldoze, and quest-wish for the best.

I'm back in the chapel, and as soon as I enter,
the wall of the stage becomes a projecting screen of fire,
which crackle-smacks one side of my face and singe-fringes my hair.
I scream, reaching past primal, and, damn it all, go bolting through
a hole in the wall.

Joke-smoky, it pretends but there are no flames in this route (none that
burn or otherwise harm me, anyway). But stumbling through mud, I turn
and catch a glimpse of a follower—the last one out from that hole.

He's chased by flames which have claimed his arms, the skin on them
blistering, peeling as he yells—the hollers only quelled when he runs
and jumps into a wet pit of mud and chud,
and rolls around
and around.

A Sister up higher, perhaps inspired, jumps from a second-story window
as flames grab for her toes and ankles. I begin to head back to help
the one Sister or other Brother, when suddenly I hear BOOM! and see
black smoke, yellow-orange-red flames shoot straight up
as four massive pillars, twenty-two feet into the air.

Judging by the area of the explosion, it's plain the flames
entered the room where we mainly stored our propane.

Uncaged and enraged, Roy's flames lick more and more pages.
And the little gadget-laden giants push more and more books of debris
into the blaze. A hogging-fog of dark first-matters: dust and gas
envelopes the scene, choking throats and hopes, racing minds backwards,
attacking dreams. A grand sound—like something produced
by warring artists performing the greatest concert of anti-music ever—
pours up with the fog: gas and engines roaring, tracks goring the earth
and scoring, wood breaking and splintering, walls crumbling and crashing
as kids still in the Center faintly scream "Mommy!" and "Daddy!" (I think.)

I consider answering, but another plan has me—
as I try to gather a clean breath, an Agent creeps up and grabs Salam,

spiriting her away from my body. I try to protest but am smacked
then kicked in the chest; an Investigator grabs my wrists, wrapping them
with unbreakable plastic strips.

                                        Jerked to my feet,
                  in a different mode,
                     resettling as I'm shoved along
—behind me, the Mound Xyn Center explodes.

Black smoke and parti-colored flames coat the sky
as the Transnational Adversary's Agents and Investigators cheer:
"Now we can go home! It's over!"
Hooray for their Independence Day.
The pyre for my Family is their smartwork of art.

My body is searched;
my free eye-thought-spirits are adrift,
searching for all that destined to be claimed by rakers
(the wonderless undertakers) of muck and ashes.
I find victims of falling concrete, vapor suffocation,
and children—too many children—whose skin burned on gas.
As they gasped for unclean, murderous air, they incessantly vomited
and choked with no choice in the matter, no voice that mattered.

For five successions of five minutes, the fire at 2000 Fahrenheit
—a height of millennial degrees. The victims, unrecognizable,
will be debated—unmistakably cremated.

The blind salamanders were delayed for four times four minutes.
From underground, maybe they came to regenerate the limbs
lost on the ground, making dismembered bodies whole (translucent
and feathered) and able to weather a brandless new life in the air.

Of us who succumbed to the services of survival (jumping out of windows,
walking through firewalls, crawling under beams, and trading the certainty
of embracing flames for the possibility of racing lead projectiles that care
nothing for names), broken limbs and third degree burns on skin
are our badges and patches for bravery in this or that combat.

Roving and reporting, I'm counting about seventy-five perished:
All of David's true flesh and blood died in the inferno; his oldest daughter,

reaching the pinnacle of six years, has been reduced to a corpse, charred,
star-burned until her body bent backwards like a bow.

Among the others, surely to be unsung: Four doves,
unloved, slung and cooked with two sticks; the demons of the flames
got fatter by feasting on two pregnant mothers and their fetuses.
Most of Xyn's children had yet to reach the leveled age of eight.
And twenty of the adults fell from life, spun, by wounds inflicted by guns.
Some shot in the back, others in the head. A few possible self-afflictions
or by peers begged by their victims to help them avoid feeling
the searing flames peel their skin. Others, who may've thought they found
the way out into the day, were sprayed by cold machines, turned up
to a high volume . . .

Escape one fire, into the rays of another.
Some valiant Siblings returned fire upon their tormentors
rather than surrender. Bend to end; spend to urn. The lesser loses.

The trapdoor to Mound Xyn's tornado shelter (a buried bus, our
immortality-extension machine, unknown and unbothered by gasses,
flames, heat, and other genocidal bothers) was weighed down by debris
from the battering-ram party; and seven lay dead in the spots,
in their labor—dismantling the pyramid of debris that was the obstacle
in the route to their savior.

Rounded up with my eight surviving Sisters and Brothers,
we're pushed onto a truck, driven to a checkpoint, hauled off, stripped,
and video-raped. Draped in orange robes (garments furthest from
the color, flavor, or status of the grape), we're forced at gunpoint back
onto the truck, stopping at a third point. Hauled off again; stripped
and searched again; then printed, redressed, and shackled.

Though we call and call, they care nothing about affairs medical.
So in pain, we continue until we reach our destination
—far beyond Waycross.

At this Adversary's station, we're split up. I lose contact with the others
—and, separate from the Family's land, I'm drained of super-spirit, far-
reaching thoughts, and extra-powered insight. I'm now reduced to feeling
and thinking of nothing but my own physical pain. Brush-ushering me
into a waiting room, along with fellow prisoners, equally broomed, I fix

my failing eyes on the television in the corner, flickering Channel 9 news.
Listening, watching there, I hear, barely, the details
of the Mound Xyn conflagration's aftermath:

"April 19th, a day of celebration for true Patriots!
Ironically, on the birthday of their untouchable patron saint,
courageous federal Agents just completed a standoff with a militia
of armed farmers popularly known as 'Xynites.'

"The Xynites are a racist cult of suicidal terrorists
that were planning a patricidal war against the federal government.
Ending today, the standoff lasted for a total of fifty days
and forty-nine nights. Rather than peacefully surrender to authorities
when given numerous chances during the whole ordeal,
the cult's leaders, we are told, convinced their brainwashed followers
to set their compound on fire, opting for mass suicide instead of a chance
at a fair trial, their day in court.

"Seventy-five of the cultists died in the self-initiated holocaust.
Of this number, twenty-five were children; and, of those twenty-five,
the thirty-three-year-old bigamist supreme cult leader, David X,
sired twelve.

"Authorities on the scene have told us they did everything they could
to save the cult members, particularly the little children. When asked
why they delayed fire trucks for a quarter of an hour at a checkpoint
—fire trucks that could've helped put the compound fire out,
possibly saving some lives—the Officials said they wanted to maintain
a distant parameter from the fire as they knew the cultists were trying
to lure them into their lair so they might burn them up too.

"One Agent who asked not to be identified by name said,
'These zealots lived out their faith to the extreme. That was their way
of getting into heaven. Why should we have run in there only to push
ourselves into sure hell, trying to make a futile attempt to prevent
what they were determined to do to themselves anyway?'

"Tonight, on the eve of his own birthday,
the President is expected to make a special speech,
praising the Agents and Investigators for their heroism
and sacrifice for the Nation."

Damned journalists:
Partisans to one heart pretending to portray art as truth
as they paint us in the imagery of old-school New Age militancy.

Skin-plumbed and inner-organs numbed, I watch from another world
as the screen shows a series of flickering pictures, film of the unrhymed
scene of the Nation's latest in a series of crimes. It's a shot
of the Family's flag, bearing its symbol of a six-pointed star
surrounded by a circle—a serpent swallowing its own tail;
on the serpent's back, are twelve little stars.

The flag is in flames, then ripped off the pole,
claimed by the legendary Texas winds.
And, with barely a moment spared, an Agent runs the standard
stars and stripes of the National Flag up the pole
in the flaming serpent's coerced absence. The last image
is of this damned fool amid black ashes, charred bones,
and a heinous sea of debris, saluting the flag
as the television plays a version of "My Country . . ."

The nefarious eagles of an iniquitous egalitarianism,
coercing all to pledge an equitable allegiance
to a sinful summing nation under some odd fraud that takes
but doesn't make.

Involuntarily, I stand up to protest,
but to make my action a jest, an Agent grabs my arm and jerks me away,
dragging me down the hall. I'm led to a room that's been darkened to pitch,
though I can see a few wisps of smoke from cigarettes being inhaled,
and I can hear scratchy whispers about someone, something
soon to be impaled.

Third-degreed: Sat in a wooden chair, illuminated,
and brusquely interrogated by four burly fellows for hours
and hours about things over which my present thoughts and memory
have no powers.

I keep asking for a lawyer; they reply
that one in my situation doesn't have that right.
I don't know what that means, so I start a varied verbal fight.

In order to get them to leave me alone
so that I might procure some rejuvenating sleep,
I begin to spin answers and then, on them, exaggerating.

But my answers have nothing to do with David, Xyn, the Family,
myself, or anything else—they are simply original doggerel, free-styled
from the dusty mental shelves.

Frustrated, they abate and have me ushered away to the front desk
near the electrical gates to be charged with weapons possession
(thirty years, possibly) and manslaughter (ten years, probably).
Officially booked, I'm officially incarcerated,
waiting for my trial date,
waiting to prove my innocence.

Home again: In a Cell.

EPILOGUE

EXTRACT FROM AN
ANTI-ESTABLISHMENT NEWLETTER

". . . no indignation at what the Nation has dug into.
Promiscuous prosecutors kiss whorish lies after death.
In the back words section of any periodical in any public library,
our greedy public servants will sell words, denying this holocaust

"that cost the lives of so many children. Not quite on the glamorous
scale of millions, but why do citizens care less, and make such a clamor
about just one kidnapped rich girl? I don't understand
why poor minorities are so hot to ignore their own while blowing kisses

"to cold authorities when they may be next on their hate list.
An unwelcome outcome.
Women whine over lost men; men sip wine over lost women.
The insipid excesses of success:
Some Muslims, a list of Christians, and a few Jews would understand.

"Veterans, mistaking the apathetic as heroic, believe
their numbers show them to be better than any lettered man or woman.
God saves by sacrificing those that are to be saved,
offering intimate relations with the sirens of fire.
But what of these three?

"David, it's said, died by a self-inflicted shot to the head.
Coroners spoke of 'a star-like explosion in the tissue.'
Escaping incineration, his right-hand man was incarcerated,
charged with baling hay. No way to bail him out of his new jail;
no way to tell if it's true that, as was reported in yesterday's news,
he hung himself with his own shoelaces in his cell. The rumor mill
has it that this occurred after he was repeatedly sodomized
with police batons.
Shoehorns or no, it still doesn't fit.

"A baby girl, the non-talking survivor of the Massacre,
is presently under the State's care. No doubt, she'll soon be claimed
by a loving family who will give her a new home and fresh name.
But for now, she has been temporarily named 'Just':

Is that short for 'Justine,' or 'Justice'?
Or just a misspelled 'Jest'?"

ABOUT THE AUTHOR

Harambee Grey-Sun is the author of three volumes of poetry and, under the name Harambee K. Grey-Sun, several works of speculative fiction. He is an alumnus of the Community of Writers at Squaw Valley. For more information about his books and ongoing projects, please visit www.harambeegreysun.com.